A WORLD OF A [illegible] AND
FA[illegible]

FOR YOU TO ENJOY !

PEDRO AND MANUEL'S ADVENTURES IN THIS WORLD AND OTHER WORLDS

P.W. MAYNARD

This book is dedicated to all children and adults with a child's heart)

Disclaimer

Do not try any of the things you read about in this book

ISBN 978-1-3999-3410-7

Excuse any mistakes I'm only human !

CHAPTER 1

Hello I am Pedro. I am eight and a half years old. I live with my grandpa Joseph in the mountains of Spain. My parents were killed in a car crash. I was staying with my grandpa when my parents were killed and stayed on with him as he is my only relative. My grandpa has helped me to overcome this sadness and to carry on with life as normal as I can.

I have to attend the local school in our village but I would sooner go into the wilds to explore. I am a born adventurer. I spend most of my time day dreaming about our fellow creatures. I have always liked all animals and my mum and dad and grandpa. I often wish I could live alone with nature in the wilds. My grandpa is not in very good health. He has worked hard all his life and is a kind man who thinks of others before himself. If he came across an animal or human in distress he would help them all he could. My teacher Miss Garcia thinks I will come to nothing in life and will probably end up as a farm labourer, but I know for sure that one day my dreams will come true. Today our lesson in school is about historical events, old battles, kings and queens. These people lived hundreds of years ago. It seems to me pointless to learn of such ancient things and the ways of the historical figures and really a waste of time in today's world and very boring. They were always fighting battles and killing each other. Couldn't they have just been kind to everyone and helped the weak and poor and animals. I'm sure they would have been happier instead of being so evil and nasty. Some wars went on for years. Couldn't they have just played golf instead? Perhaps not, if one of them lost the game the loser would probably hit the other one on the head with a golf club if they had golf then.

My teacher's father is the local mayor Alfonso Garcia, a short fat man who thinks he is the local Lord of the land. My grandfather says he's not a very nice man. He does have a look of a donkey with a tummy ache. "Oh great, the school bell has rung. School finished for the day.

I live about a couple of kilometres outside of our village. My grandfather's house is a bit run down but I don't care because it's cosy and homely. He has chickens and an old goat called Matilda.

He named her after my grandmother who died 9 years ago. I don't remember her.

I share my room with a cat called Piggy. I named her that because she eats anything. Grandpa says she's a dustbin on four legs.

I hope my grandpa lives a long time. He is great. He lets me do as I want and I suppose I just run wild to the annoyance of many people in the village, but I just love nature and love to care for it. Even if I see a worm in the road I have to pick it up and put it safely in the grass.

"Pedro !"

That is my grandfather calling – "Coming Grandpa" "Its time for tea." Said Grandpa.

My grandpa isn't exactly a first class chef. We seem to live on eggs on toast and a couple of lettuce leaves out of the garden. But one thing we do have which I love is fruit. There are all sorts of fruit trees – orange, plum, cherry, apple, pear, figs and grape vines. So lovely to pick fresh and warm straight from the tree or bush.

In my room I have a mattress on the floor stuffed with straw and a piece of string nailed to two walls for my clothes to hang on. We have only an old wireless for company, which my grandpa doesn't seem to like too much and if it doesn't work properly he hits it on the top and it seems to get it going again.

Since coming to live with my grandpa and living quite a way from the village I didn’t bother with friends from school and just made all of nature my friend. I even have a couple of little lizards who when its cold slide under my blanket on the mattress for warmth. They often move about and tickle my feet.

A field mouse gets under my blanket also. He is very sweet and I like to tell him a story. He comes in every night. I know he doesn’t understand my stories but he likes to lie on top of the blanket and stare at me. He has become very tame as I give him some biscuit and cheese. I call him “messy” because he leaves little mouse droppings on the floor. I haven’t house trained him yet. Matilda our goat wakes me up every morning with a lick on my head and her wet whiskers dripping on my face. It's my job to milk and feed her so there's no chance of a lie in. She lives in the house at night with us because there are wolves in the mountains which might eat her. Our chickens come in the house at night also because of foxes. What with lizard, mouse, goat and chickens indoors it's like a zoo. I think if my grandpa ran the world there would be changes and no animals would suffer again under man's evil nature. Why do we treat animals so badly? They are our fellow creatures. We wouldn't treat children like that, so why our fellow creatures?

I have a friend in the next village called Manuel. He's a lot older than me. He's 25 but because something went wrong when he was born he has the mental age of a small child. But he loves all animals. He is a gentle giant over 6ft 10" tall and very strong. One day a few months ago he was crossing the road when a car driving too fast hit him, but he got up straight away and put his hand under the car and turned it upside down. I think that may have taught the driver to drive slowly in future. Manuel just walked away and sat on the wall opposite as if nothing had happened. When the local police arrived the car driver said "arrest that lunatic – he turned my car over with me in it". The police officer took one look at Manuel sitting on the wall and said to the driver “you are under arrest for possible driving while drunk. I’ve heard some stories before but this beats them all”. The driver was still protesting while being put in the police car. The only person who saw what happened was me and I’m not telling!

“Come on Manuel; let’s go to the hills to find the deer. They are at low levels at this time of year and in a playful mood. Its fun to watch them!

Lots of wild animals will come to Manuel and let him touch them. He loves this. He never stops smiling when this happens. They must sense he is kind and will do them no harm. On one occasion we were sitting in a meadow in a wild part of a valley when a pack of wolves came towards us. I was scared but Manuel just put out his hand and the wolves came up to him and licked his hand and lay down by him. Manuel stroked them one at a time. They acted like puppies. If I had told anyone of what had happened no one would believe me. That's the way animals react to him. It's so lovely to see. No sooner had they come to Manuel they just got up and walked away but one of the wolves turned around to look back at us and gave a soft howling noise as if to say goodbye to Manuel. "Come on Manuel" I said we had better get going home or your mother Sophia will be worried. Manuel barely talks but always smiles. His mother once said to me "please don’t leave the area as Manuel would be so upset if you did”. I told Sophia “I will always be there for Manuel. He is my kindred spirit and a brother I never had”

CHAPTER 2

We arrived back in Manuel’s village and Sophia was waiting for him. “Come on Manuel, your tea is ready. Pedro would you like to stay for tea?” “Oh yes please. Real good home cooking instead of grandfather’s egg on toast” I said. “Will your grandfather mind?”

“If you stay will he be worried?”

“No, I don’t think so. He’s probably having an afternoon nap which lasts for hours sometimes. He sounds like a pig snoring. It’s so loud.” Sophia made a fish pie with vegetables from the garden. It smells yummy. Perhaps if I move in with Manuel and Sophia, grandfather might not miss me then I could have lovely meals each day but Grandfather would be very lonely and have nobody to cook his famous egg on toast for me! It was so good I ate it quickly and got hiccups. “Thank you very much for that lovely feast Sophia”. “You’re very welcome Pedro. Come as often as you like. We always have plenty to eat ?

“I had better get back to Grandfather it is getting very late.” As I went, Manuel just gave a huge smile and waved. “See you tomorrow Manuel” I said.

It took about 15 minutes to get home just before dark. “Hello Pedro” said grandfather. “Tea will soon be ready. I expect you are hungry. “Oh yes grandpa I can’t wait. Oh dear I thought. I am full up. I know - when grandpa isn’t looking I will give most of my meal to Matilda our old goat. She eats anything. But when grandpa put the food on the table, I was shocked because it was real food with fresh crusty bread. Grandpa smiled and said “it’s not as good as my egg on toast because the hens are not laying today for some reason. Still, it will fill you up”. Even though I was full up with Sophia’s meal I found room for this rare meal from grandpa. “Sorry Matilda its all mine!”

Only a few days to go before the school holiday! Five weeks with no boring lessons on subjects. Great! Manuel and I can spend lots of time in the valley and hills. This is where we learn of real life in the beauty of it all. After those two meals I felt really tired. “Goodnight grandpa – I want to go to bed now”. “O.K. Pedro. Sweet dreams”.

Just as I got into bed it started to rain hard. It has not rained for a long time and the air smelt sweet. I was just going to put the light out when I saw a mouse. "Oh hello, Mr Mouse. It's horrible and wet outside. Come and sleep under my blanket to keep warm and safe. Goodnight Mr Mouse. Sleep tight and don't let the bed bugs bite. Sorry I can't tell you a story tonight, I'm so tired – goodnight". I didn't know what time it was but it was dark and I was woken up by a strange noise like someone eating. I turned on the light. "Oh Matilda. Are you scared of the rain too?" Eat up your cabbage leaves and go to sleep". I would probably get more peace if I slept in a zoo. "Goodnight everyone and you too piggy".

The next morning the rain had gone and it was as usual a clear blue sky. "Get up Pedro shouted grandpa". "O.k. Grandpa. Hello Mr Mouse. Did you sleep well? You can have a lie in if you want. I've got to go to school and learn a lot of things." "Here Pedro, eat this sandwich on your way to school as you are late. "Thanks grandpa. Oh no, not egg sandwich. One day I will turn into a chicken. Still I might be able to swop my sandwich at school with a chocolate bun or anything but an egg sandwich."

On my way towards the village and school I met a very old man who had a huge white beard. " Never seen you before" I said. "Do you live far away?" "Yes I do. I lived in Barcelona and always wanted to be at one with nature. Though I fear I may have left it a bit late as I'm 89 this year. "Wow you still look fit and walk without a stick. Not like most old people". "Thank you. And to whom am I talking to ""I am Pedro. I live in the wilds with my grandpa." "What's your name"? "I am Gonzalez ". "What's in your back pack? It looks big "

"That's my sleeping bag and a few bits said Gonzalez. I sleep under the stars. It's so lovely. "Have you eaten today" "No, I get food where I can. Sometimes fruit from the trees and some kind folk give me something to eat. "Oh, I forgot school – I must rush. "Here, have my lovely fresh egg sandwich". "Thank you Pedro but wont you miss this lovely sandwich said Gonzalez. "No, I think I can miss it just this once! “Will you be around here after school? I said. “Yes I will be over there by the almond trees”. “Okay, goodbye “

Miss Garcia my teacher says we must work hard and get a good job; get a pension plan for our old age’; save for a rainy day. It only rains around here about twice a year so I won’t have to save much. I am only 8 so why do I want to save for a pension plan. I’m not retiring for donkey’s years. Besides I don’t want to be like all the other people working on a giant hamster wheel missing the beauty of real living with nature for a pension of peanuts. That’s what my grandpa says – my entire pension is just peanuts. People are like robots. They forget we live in a lovely world full of the beauty of life and nature. Everyone should take a long, long break from the hamster wheel and find out how wonderful it is out there." "Pedro! "Yes Miss Garcia" "You have been daydreaming again. Did you know the bell has rung?" All the other children have gone home"!

"Oh yes – oops. Bye see you tomorrow". "No you won't – its Saturday Pedro" "Great!"

On my way back home I stopped near to the almond trees. The old man Senor Gonzalez was lying on the ground and not moving. I said out loud "I wonder if he's dead! "No, I'm not – I'm just having a snooze". "Oh that's good. Have you had a good day?" said Pedro "Yes lovely just pure almond blossom scent and peace" said Gonzalez. "Oh that's good.

"Would you like to come and have tea with me and Grandpa?"

"That would be lovely. Will your Grandpa mind?" "No, he would love to have someone of a similar age to talk to. "Is he 89?" "No but he looks like it. Let me help you up" "Thank you Pedro." "It's not far just over that hill. We walked along in peaceful silence and then arrived home. Here we are. "Grandpa where are you? Oh, I can hear him in the barn trying to milk Matilda. Sounds like his usual naughty words when Matilda won't keep still. I don't think calling Matilda names will help." Grandpa we have a visitor! This is Senor Gonzalez. He's travelling and enjoying nature. "Hello I'm Joseph." "Can Senor Gonzalez stay for tea? I think he's hungry. "Of course. Come in and rest your bones "said Joseph.

"What a lovely homely house you have. Plain and comfortable without the usual trappings of most people. Filling a house with useless trinkets and stupid ornaments". "I totally agree with you Senor. People spend their lives collecting things and filling a house with useless expensive junk. The happiest people I know have very little and are not shackled with useless possessions”.

“Pedro can you finish milking Matilda so we can have a glass of milk with our tea.”? “O.k. Grandpa.”

“He’s a good boy Gonzales but I fear what will happen to him if I die soon.” “Joseph, I wouldn’t worry about that. From what I’ve seen of him and his philosophy of life he will be just fine. He is a born adventurer. I think he will do more in his life than both of us have done.” “Thank you Senor. That helps my mind.” “Here we are fresh milk” said Pedro. “How is it Matilda is good with you but not with me.” “Well Grandpa I don’t use naughty words. I think it upsets her. What's for tea grandpa."? Well we have goats cheese which is now ready to eat. Home baked bread and fresh vegetables soup". "That looks wonderful Joseph said Gonzalez - what a feast! " "Enjoy it senor". After our meal grandpa and senor Gonzalez started to talk about the old days. I'm too young to talk about the old days so I went to bed in my room. I could hear them talking and laughing. It was good to hear my grandpa having a good time. He probably gets lonely and someone to talk to of his own age is good, the next morning I was woken by Piggy the cat wanting her breakfast. She wakes me up at the same time each morning. I'm sure she has got a watch!

I woke late the next morning. “Good Morning Grandpa. Where is Senor Gonzalez?” “He’s gone. He wanted to set out early because he has a long walk to the next village over the hills” why didn’t he say goodbye to me. Did I upset him? “No he said it makes him sad to say goodbye to a kindred spirit like you. But he will always remember you and your kindness. I’m sad too because I was going to ask him how long it took to grow his beard. Probably all his life. It was very big and bushy. Well it’s Saturday. What are you up to today Pedro?” “Well when I’ve done my chores I’m going to see Manuel. Sophia asked me last week if I would help Manuel with his reading and writing. He doesn’t know many words but Sophia thinks he might take notice of me. Other people have tried but soon lose patience and shout at him which is very stupid. He can't help the way he was born. Anyway grandpa I'm out all day. Sophia is giving me lunch for helping Manuel". "You have a good kind heart and spirit Pedro" "Thank you grandpa but I think all well and able people should count themselves lucky and help those who are not so lucky in life". "That's a good philosophy Pedro. I'm proud of you. What time are you coming home?" About five. Bye grandpa"

CHAPTER 3

On my way to Manuel's I was thinking how lucky was. I don't have much but we live in a beautiful wild countryside full of life and trees and flowers. The air is clean and pure and we don't have any fear of crime. I wonder how many millions of people who are very rich but are not content and just want more would love to have our peace and joy. Something no amount of money can buy.

I arrived at Manuel's house. The front door was open. "Hello anyone home? "Yes Pedro just come in. Manuel doesn't like his hair washed so I told him you were coming for the day and he had to look clean and tidy. There he is clean as a new born lamb. You can use the dining table to teach Manuel some more words. There are some plain paper sheets on the table and two pens”.

I had just started to show Manuel pictures in a book to help explain simple useful words when there was a crash in the kitchen and then silence. I went out to see what had happened and on the floor not moving was Sophia. Are you O.K.? ? Not a word. What shall I do I thought. “Manuel come quickly! Pick up Sophia and put her on her bed. Just sit by her and hold her hand. I’m going to get Dr Rodriquez.”

I ran to the doctor’s house and banged on the door. I could hear a voice. “Just coming said the doctor. "You don't have to bash the door down! Ah hello Pedro. What's the matter?"

"Please come quickly. Sophia is ill. She fell on the floor"
"Just let me grab by medicine bag. Come on".

When we got to Sophia's house Manuel was still holding Sophia's hand. He was just staring and sitting totally still like he was frozen.

"It's probably shock said Dr Rodriquez. Let me check Sophia out".

Dr Rodriquez put his ear thing to Sophia's heart. "Her heart is still working O.K. But her breathing is a bit slow".

"Pedro go and get a clean cloth and wet with cold water". "Here you are Dr Sanchez". "Right I'll just lay it on her forehead. I'm not surprised something like this has happened. It must be very stressful looking after Manuel." Just then Sophia sat up. Manuel was still holding her hand and tears were running down his face. "Its o.k. Manuel said the doctor. Sophia will soon be better with a rest for a few days. I will get my wife Maria to stay and keep an eye on her until she can cope. It would help Pedro if you would stay the night as well. It would help Manuel to have a good friend with him”. “Yes I will” said Pedro.

“I’m going by your house later. I will tell your Grandpa Joseph what has happened” said the doctor. Sophia said “don’t make so much fuss. I will be fine in a while”. “Just to be safe Sophia Maria will help you get some rest and cook you and Manuel some food and stay the night. Tomorrow you may feel much better and she may not need to stay much longer. I will go now and Maria will be over shortly.”

“I’ve caused a bit of a problem calling Dr Rodriquez and now Maria is coming over. Thank you for staying Pedro. It will help so much for Manuel to have you here" said Sophia. Manuel was still looking a bit shocked,

"Here's Maria. "Hello Sophia," "I'm sorry to be such a nuisance .Maria". "Don't be silly Sophia. It's the least I can do to help. It's a sad world if we can't help one another. Right you two boys go and get some logs. I will light a fire its gets a bit chilly at night and Sophia needs to be kept warm. Come on Manuel lets get some logs". Soon the fire was roaring and Maria had made some chicken soup for Sophia and a pie for Manuel and me. I don't know what was in the pie but it was lovely. It was getting late and Maria said "I think you boys should get ready for bed.

Sophia is now resting after her soup and I expect will soon be asleep. "

"Come on Manuel. After we are ready for bed I will tell you a story like I tell to my pet Mousie Messy. I expect he wonders where I am. Still when I go home I will give him a big piece of cheese. That should cheer him up."

Manuel was on his bed and I had an old mattress on the floor. Manuel still looked a bit shocked so I just put out the light. I don't think he would want a story at this time.

CHAPTER 4

The next morning Manuel was not in his bed. I got dressed and saw him in Sophia's room holding her hand again. Maria was in the kitchen getting breakfast. "Sophia is much better today Pedro". "That's good. Manuel will be pleased to see Sophia back to normal. I don't suppose he really understands what is going on or perhaps he does in his sweet child like way. "I expect your grandpa will have missed you last night. How is he these days? It's a while since I visited him." Sometimes he seems fine and sometimes he looks unwell and in deep thought. He's a good man but he has had a hard life and not taken too much care of his body. Still he has you to look after so that you keep his going. If you want to go home all is well here."

"I suppose I should go but a bit later I want to make sure Manuel is okay and happy again". Maria ruffled my hair and said "What a good kind boy you are" And I had only just combed my hair. Now I have to comb it again. I went to see Sophia. She was sitting in a chair now and looking much better. "It's nice to see you well" I said. "Thank you Pedro". "Come on Manuel. Let's go outside and find some lizards". Manuel let go of Sophia's hand and looked at her and smiled and came with me outside. As we sat outside on the wall we didn't get much chance to catch lizards because every villager that went by wanted to know how Sophia was. I had to tell each one what had happened and by the time I told the story so many times my throat was sore. One nice old lady came up and kissed Manuel on the cheek and gave him a bar of chocolate and when she was gone he put the bar in my hand and said "you have it". I was a bit shocked. He very rarely say's anything. I just smiled and thanked him and broke the bar in two and said "you have some too". We both enjoyed the chocolate. It was a real treat as Grandpa doesn't have much money so I only get chocolate at Christmas. Manuel looked his normal self now so I said I had to go soon as Grandpa might need some chores done. I took Manuel indoors to see Sophia.

He went straight to see Sophia and sat by her side and just looked at her with a big smile. "Goodbye Sophia, Manuel. I'm off home now. "Goodbye and thank you Pedro. You are a credit to your grandfather. He would always help anyone in need. You must have his goodness. "Bye Manuel" I said. Manuel just waved. It didn't take long to get home and grandpa was sitting on the porch. He was snoozing in his rocking chair and had a straw hat on and Matilda was trying to reach his hat probably to eat it and I started to laugh out loud. It woke grandpa up. "What's that" he said. “It’s only me grandpa, Pedro”. “It’s nice to have you home. Is everything alright with Sophia”? Yes she is much better and Dr Rodriguez wife is keeping an eye on them”. “That’s good news. Are you hungry”? Oh yes, I am. I forgot about food this morning and I didn’t like to ask for some as they were all too busy being happy. “I’ve made some goat’s milk yogurt. Would you like it with chopped fruit in”? Said grandpa.

“Yes please grandpa”.

“I’ve got some news you will like. Your teacher Miss Garcia has a bad cold or flu and so the school holidays will start early.” “Wow, what great news. “ “I thought you would be pleased". Said Grandpa. "Did you hear that Matilda. No school for 5 weeks and 3 days. Hip hip hooray".

"What are you going to do with your time in the holidays Pedro"?

"Well grandpa if Sophia is totally better Manuel and I want to explore the valley of rocks for a start. I remember playing there as a child with my dog Happy." "Why did you call him Happy? Said grandpa"

"Because no matter how sad I was his tail would wag and wag and he was always happy. So I thought that was a good name for him. I don't have a dog now but I have my friend Manuel and he is usually happy".

Grandpa said last year I could have a dog but I would have to brush it and look after it and clean up after it. "I do like dogs although I think other people's dogs are best. You pat them and play with them and you don't have to pick up their mess."

"Pedro can you get some logs in for tonight. Its going to be a pit chilly" said Grandpa. It feels still very hot to me. I think grandpa's body gets cold quick. He says it happens in old age. I'm glad grandpa told me that. I will just buy a big coat when I get old and wear it all day. It will keep me nice and warm and I

won't have to get logs. "Pedro its time you had a bath" said Grandpa. "Not again grandpa. I had one a few days ago."
"Well its time for another. Cleanliness is next to Godliness Pedro."

"Oh, I suppose you are right Grandpa. Every time I see a picture of God he's always got a white robe on so he must wash a lot. If I wash a lot like God will I look white and shiny?"
"God doesn't have to bath because he is clean and pure" said Grandpa. "Oh does that mean he gets other people to do his chores so he doesn't get dirty?" "Probably - now Just get the bath ready Pedro. "

After I had a bath Grandpa had the fire going. It was lovely and he toasted some bread on it and we put some wild honey on it. Yummy! "Millions of people who are starving around the world Pedro would love to eat our simple meal" said Grandpa. "Why are so many people starving Grandpa?"

"Well mostly because the world is run by greedy people who have no compassion for anyone suffering. They only care about getting more and more money which they hoard. They will never be able to spend it. They could help the starving but they don't because with greed comes a sickness of the mind.

“Couldn’t they take a tablet to cure it Grandpa? “ I questioned

“No amount of tablets will cure them.”

“I don’t think I want to be rich grandpa. I would sooner just eat our simple food and have the gift of joy and nature.”

“Would you like to play dominoes for a while before going to bed?

“Yes please Grandpa. While I was away did you see my little mouse?

“Yes he came in and sat on your mattress and curled up. I think he missed you. I gave him a piece of cheese and told him you would be back soon.” replied Grandpa.

“Oh good. Thanks for feeding him. I don’t want him to starve. He is my friend. I shall always remember times like these. A log fire, some toast and a grown up game of dominoes. What fun Grandpa”

“You look like you can hardly keep your eyes open. It’s time for bed”.

“I do feel very sleepy. Goodnight grandpa.”

“Goodnight. Here’s a little piece of toast for your mouse. I expect he would like some supper.”

CHAPTER 5

When I opened the door to my room Piggy was sitting right in the middle of my mattress. “Come on get off. Your place is over there in the straw “.

As I got into bed and got all cosy my friend Messy mouse climbed onto the mattress. “Hello. Did you miss me? I’ll tell you all about my day. Here’s some toast. Have a feast.” I started to tell Messy about how today went. The next I remember was waking up in the morning.

"That was a lovely night's sleep grandpa! "Yes I know I heard you snoring.

"I don't snore. You must have heard your echo" I said.

"Oh I forgot to tell you Don Sebastian is going up to the posh ski resort to deliver some furniture for the ski chalets. He thought you might like a trip to the mountains to see the snow and see how the rich live. He's coming by at about 10.30. Would you like to go?" "Yes please Grandpa" I said.

"You don't need to take any sandwiches Don will treat you to a meal in one of the restaurants. Put some clean clothes on and brush your hair. You don't want to look like a street urchin and don't forget to wash behind your ears." said Grandpa.

"What's the point of washing there? Nobody can see" I said.
"Just do it Pedro!"

"Its 10.30 Grandpa and he's not here".

"Be patient. Looking at the clock won't make him get here any quicker." Just at that moment I heard a toot toot. "Here he comes." I exclaimed.

Hello Joseph. Hello Pedro. Do you want to come for a ride to the snow? "Oh yes please

Don! " "We will be back about 6 this evening Joseph"

"Right Pedro hop in the cab."

"I've never been in a big lorry before. It feels so high up". "Right off we go. Bye grandpa. See you tonight."

"Take care. Enjoy your day Pedro and do what Don says." Said Grandpa.

"He's a good lad Joseph. He will be fine." I waved to grandpa until I could see him no more. As we went along Don said "You are quiet. Are you o.k.? "Oh yes I'm just enjoying looking at the beautiful countryside and thinking about all the animals that live in peace away from humans."

"I agree with you Pedro. But not all humans are horrible to animals. There are lots of people who look out for them. You hear about all the horrible things going on in this world but hardly anything about all the good things. "

"It sounds interesting but I didn't understand much"

Just keep away from the world and its woes and enjoy your love of nature. Tens of millions would love to live where we are in tune with the natural world".

“Look can you see the big hotel in the distance? That’s where we are going. We will be there in a few minutes. We arrived and Don backed up to the delivery entrance to unload the furniture for the guest chalets. It will take about 2 hours to unload. Do you want to sit in the cab? Said Don.

“Can I go for a walk and see the people ski. “

“Yes sure. But don’t go too far and remember where I am. If you get a bit lost say you want to get to the hotel plaza. Don’t worry I wont leave without you” said Don.
“Look at all the snow. How do the animals get food? Said Pedro.

“Perhaps the hotel gives them the scraps that are left.” Replied Don.

“I have never seen so many people in such a small area. They look rich with big cars and lovely clothes.” People were sitting outside a café. Some of the ladies had fur coats on and I said “excuse me is your coat real animal fur? “Yes it is. Why do you want to know? Said the lady.

“Well I have lots of animal friends with fur. I hope it’s not one of them you have on”
“Oh go away boy. Animals are there to be eaten and wear their skins” the lady replied.

“No they are not. They are our friends and you shouldn’t hurt a friend.” I said.

“Just go away boy.” said the woman.

What horrible people I thought. All they seem to care about are themselves. I’m glad I don’t belong in their world with no love and compassion for animals. I really thought I would love to see this place of snow and nice things but I can’t wait to go home now to be with really kind human beings who have very little but are totally happy.

“Pedro come. I’ve finished unloading quicker than I thought. Have you had a good time?”

“No the people here seem to be rich are not kind.. Can we go home now?

“Don’t you want some food?

“Yes but not here.”

“I will get some sandwiches then. We will have a picnic out in the wild.” said Don.

CHAPTER 6

We travelled for about an hour before Don pulled over. "Come on Pedro. There's a lovely place over there with lovely views and total peace. Now would you like cheese or ham? Cheese thank you Don". I have no money to pay for the sandwich." "Don't be silly Pedro. You don't have to pay. It's my treat for having your company today and when you have finished your sandwich there's some chocolate cake."

"Thank you. Wow a real feast."

"You are passionate about animals aren't you? When did it start? Said Don. "Well when I came to live with Grandpa and on my 5th birthday he took me to a circus. The animals were kept in small cages which made me sad because they should be free to live their lives. I told grandpa it made me upset to see them having to do stupid tricks then put back into a cage. I had to get out of the circus tent. As we walked past a cage on the back of a lorry a bear was just sitting and staring at the forest across the road. I don't know why but I ran over to the cage and Grandpa said

“Pedro come away. It’s a dangerous animal”. The bear looked me in the eyes. I could feel its sadness. I put my hand on the cage. The bear gently moved its paw to touch my hand. Grandpa saw the bear was very gentle.
“Pedro you must be a kindred spirit to animals. They must sense your child like innocence and compassion.”

Its makes me very angry to see this lovely animal living like this I told Grandpa. The padlock on the cage was not locked properly so I said
“Can we let it go? That would be a lovely thing to give it its freedom.”
“But it might attack us said Grandpa”.

“No grandpa I can see in its eyes it would not hurt us” I said.

“Okay but I must be mad. Here goes.” We took the lock off and opened the cage. Grandpa said “Pedro come away”. “No I have to show him the way to freedom. Come Mr Bear this way. There are the woods. Get as far away as you can into the wilds.”

The bear ran over to the woods and stopped. It turned around and looked at me for a moment then disappeared. Will he get food grandpa” I said.

“Yes his natural instinct will take over. Quick lets go before we get caught letting out a circus animal.”

“He’s not just an animal grandpa. He’s a fellow creature who needed help. My friend Manuel has a wonderful way with animals. Better than me. They all take to him like they have known him forever. It’s so nice to watch although I always like animals and wanted to help them it was Manuel’s magic way with them. If Manuel had let the bear out of the cage it would have probably licked his face in gratitude!

It was then that I realised I had to help any fellow creatures in distress.”

"I wonder if the bear is still out there Pedro" said Don.

"I hope so. There's a lot of wilderness for him to be safe in."

"You've made me think Pedro. It is cruel to keep any animal or bird in a cage. They belong in the hills and valleys and woods to enjoy their lives. Everyone deserves to live the lives they were created for. Come on Pedro. Let's go home."

When we arrived at Grandpas house he was sitting on the porch.

“Thank you Don for giving Pedro a nice day out. We don’t go far. I cannot afford to go on trips with Pedro though I would like to.”

“It was a pleasure to have Pedro’s company. I didn’t think when I set out this morning to come over to pick him up that I would learn from him at his age a lesson in kindness to animals. Thank you again. Next time I go somewhere in the wilds on a delivery Pedro can come with me again. Would you like that Pedro?

“Yes please.” “Right I must get home now. Bye bye.”

We waved to Don as he drove off. Grandpa then said “Pedro I have some sad news for you. Sophia has died. She didn’t suffer. It was quick. Dr Rodriguez said it was a heart attack.”

“How is Manuel? I said. “He is taking it badly and won’t let anyone near his mother after Dr Rodriguez left. I think at this time you are the only one who can comfort him.” said Grandpa.

“I’m going over to see him now Grandpa.”

“You’ve had a long day.” Said Grandpa

“I don’t mind. It’s my friend Manuel I’m worried about.”

As I walked over to the village it was unusually quiet. I expect the villagers were shocked. Dr Rodriguez saw me. “Pedro do you know what’s happened?” “Yes Grandpa told me. I’ve come to comfort my friend Manuel.”

“Good you have wisdom beyond your years.” Said Dr Rodriguez.

“What will happen to Manuel? He only had his mother” I said.

“Well he may have to go into a home to be looked after.” Said Dr Rodriguez.

“No. he will come to live with us. Grandpa wouldn’t let Manuel be taken away.

“That’s wonderful. I was hoping that might happen. I’ll leave you to comfort him”. Said Dr Rodriguez.

As I walked into Manuel’s house I could see him through the door holding Sophia’s hand. Tears were running down his face. I sat beside him and touched his hand. He looked at me and stared into my eyes.

“Don’t worry Manuel, Grandpa and I will take care of you.”

I stayed with him that night. We didn't get much sleep. The next day Dr Rodriguez came back with the local undertaker. "How is Manuel Pedro.?

"He seems to be in another world." "Tell him we will have to lay Sophia to rest. It's best coming from you"

I put my hand on his hand. "Manuel Dr Rodriguez has to take Sophia to a place to be buried and then she will go to heaven and one day you will see her again. " At first Manuel would not let go of her hand. Then suddenly he looked at me and smiled. He then kissed his mother's head and waved goodbye to her. I held his hand and told him that he would come and live with us now. “Grandpa will put another mattress in my room so we can share the room and you won’t be alone. “

Manuel held my hand tight and we started to go home. A lot of villagers came out and said “bless you Manuel and bless you Pedro.” We carried on up the hill towards home. On the way back I started to think about Manuel having the mind of a small child in a man’s body. In some ways at this time it may have been a blessing. As we got to Grandpa’s house Matilda and Piggy came up to Manuel and he stroked them and picked piggy up. Piggy doesn’t usually like that but was happy to be in Manuel’s arms. Piggy seemed to comfort Manuel so my grumpy old cat has a good side after all.

That evening we all sat around the fire. Manuel just stared into the flames. Piggy lay down by Manuel's chair and so did Matilda. I have heard many people say that farm animals have no intelligence but they have something far far better – love and compassion. Something that seems to be missing in our fast paced me, me, me world.

Manuel was starting to doze in the chair so Grandpa said "Come on you two. Off to bed. You are both looking tired out." We went into my room. Manuel looked around. I think he was still in shock. "This is your room as well Manuel. We can be like brothers. Manuel smiled and we got ready for bed. “Just before I put the light out Manuel I had better let you know I have a pet mouse called Messy. He comes in about now. I’ve saved him a biscuit to eat.”

As Manuel never says very much I was surprised when he said. “I like mice.” “Goodnight Manuel I hope tomorrow you feel a little better. As I lay there I noticed Manuel had gone to sleep quickly. Just then Messy climbed onto my mattress. “Hello I said “we have got a new room mate. Don’t worry messy he looks big but he loves animals. When he’s better I will tell him about you and you can be his friend too. He will want to give you a biscuit too. With two biscuits a day you might get a bit fat."

I lay my head on the pillow and before I went to sleep I noticed Piggy and Matilda had sneaked in and lay down by Manuel.

"Goodnight everyone. Sleep tight. Don't let the bed bugs bite"

CHAPTER 7

When I woke up the next morning Manuel was not there. I got up and dressed. Grandpa was getting breakfast. “Where’s Manuel?” I said.

“He’s out on the porch in the rocking chair. Leave him alone for a while with his thoughts”.

After grandpa had made breakfast he told me to get Manuel. “He must be hungry by now. I don’t suppose he ate much yesterday.” said Grandpa.

“No we both didn’t.” I said. I made some toast with cheese on and some freshly cooked ginger biscuits with a nice cold glass of milk. We both tucked in like we had never eaten before. We must have been hungrier than we thought. Soon it was all gone.

“Well you two that didn’t take long to eat” said Grandpa.

“That was lovely Grandpa.

“Why don’t you take Manuel into the wilds today? He likes to see the various animals. I’ll make some sandwiches and lemonade.”

“Thanks grandpa. What a feast. Manuel do you want to go for a picnic and watch all your animal friends? He looked at me and said yes. “He seems to be getting more at ease with us Grandpa.”

“That’s great. One day we might have a good talk together.” said Grandpa.

“Bye Grandpa” I said as we set off and to my surprise Manuel turned around and waved to Grandpa. “Goodbye you two take care. Don’t do anything silly”. “No we won’t. See you later”

After a few kilometres Manuel pointed to a grassy meadow where wild flowers were swaying in the breeze. “Why don’t you sit there Manuel” Manuel found a fallen tree trunk to sit against. It was a beautiful day not a cloud in the sky. Bees were busy on the flowers. Skylarks were singing high up in the sky. Just then Manuel pointed to the sky. “Look Sophia!”

He looked so happy I could not see anything but he must have. Perhaps only close children can see their loved ones. A great peace seemed to come over Manuel. He looked like his old self again. I don't know what had happened but it seems to have given him peace of mind. For a long time he just gazed into the sky with a smile on his face. To my surprise he suddenly said "bye Moma see you soon". They were some of the longest words I have heard Manuel use. Something good seemed to be coming out of all the sadness. I could still not see anything but I waved into the sky. "Bye Sophia." At that moment a voice said "take care of my baby". It was so quick I thought I was hearing things. But then I realised the voice was just like Sophia's calm and soft voice. Now I was staring into the sky with Manuel. I gave Manuel a hug. He just smiled with a look of happiness. “Shall we just stay here for the day Manuel?” He just said “yes please”.

We had our sandwiches and with the sun lovely and warm we must have dozed off. I woke up and just in front of me was a wolf. “Manuel wake up. Don’t move. We had better stay still. He might hurt us. “ Then Manuel just said “my friend”. Then I remembered the wolf he stroked in the valley a while ago which was part of a pack. Manuel put his hand out and the wolf came to him and licked his face.

I thought I was having a dream but when the wolf licked my hand I knew I wasn't. I couldn't believe what had happened. Does the wolf know of Manuel's sadness and wants to comfort him I wondered? I think we humans know nothing about how loving animals really are. If we just stopped hunting them and treating them in horrible ways they would trust us and really become our friends. I think Grandpa is right when he says anyone who hurts animals is evil and doesn't deserve to be alive. The wolf just sat by Manuel's side like a puppy dog.

"What are you going to call him Manuel? He needs a name now he's your friend."

Manuel looked at the wolf and said "Mr Wolf." "Well it's good he's a big good wolf and not a big bad wolf" I said.

Through the long grass suddenly a lot of wolves came and stopped and lay down and stared at us. Mr Wolf got up and licked Manuel once more. Manuel touched Mr Wolf on the back and stroked him. Mr Wolf looked into Manuel's eyes. His nose was almost touching Manuel's nose. He stared for a few minutes then walked to his wolf friends and they walked away. At the end of the meadow was a rock. Mr Wolf climbed onto it and looked back at us. We both said "bye bye Mr Wolf" and laughed with joy. "See you again".

The wolves then went into the woods at the end of the meadow. “I can’t wait to tell Grandpa about this when we get home” I said. “He’s probably the only one who will believe us.” As we got up there was a lot of bird song. I have never heard so much. It was like an orchestra of song. There were also deer and rabbits and lots of other animals looking at us. I think they have come to tell Manuel all is well now.

“Come Manuel lets go home and tell grandpa about our lovely day with our fellow creatures.”

Just as we got up to go a strong wind started to blow over the meadow. All the flowers and grasses were waving about in the wind. It looked like they were waving us goodbye. “We had better wave back to the flowers Manuel otherwise they will think we don’t like them”. Manuel started to wave at the flowers and grasses. “Pedro you wave too.” “Okay I said as we waved and laughed. “What a wonderful day after all that’s happened. Grandpa always says every day is a wonderful day if you live with the beauty of nature all around you. If you live in big cities with no nature to see and no lovely fresh air it must be like a prison of noise and soulless humans rushing around with no time for anybody except for themselves. How sad they think that they have everything but really they have nothing but a soulless life away from the beauty of nature."

"There's grandpa in the garden. "Hello you two" he said. Have you had some fun today?" "If you come in and sit down Grandpa we will tell you about a day you won't believe!"

We told grandpa all that had happened. "I believe you two. I have seen and heard of people in contact with so called wild animals and many stories of how these animals helped humans in need or after a human had helped an animal. I had a friend when I was young. His name was Daniel. He moved to America and one day on his way home from work he cut across some derelict land for a short cut to his house. As he passed an old tin shed he heard a whining sound coming from it. On opening the door he found a large Alsatian dog in a bad way. I think he got in there and couldn't get out. He wondered how long he had been there. Daniel gave the dog a beef sandwich which he had not eaten at work. The dog ate it like he was starving. "If you come home with me I will help you to get better" said Daniel. The dog got up a bit wobbly and followed Daniel out of the tin hut. "Come on I will walk slowly so that you can keep up." The dog walked behind Daniel. When he got home Daniel found an old bowl and filled it with water. The dog drank lots. "I don't know if I've got much dog type food in the house. Oh I know I have some tins of corned beef.” Daniel put the contents of two tins into a bowl. The dog ate the lot in about 10 seconds. “Wow you are hungry. Come and lie by the fire.” Said Daniel. The dog lay by the fire and went to sleep. “You must be exhausted poor thing”.

As the days past Daniel cleaned the dog, fed him good food and two weeks passed. The dog looked in lovely condition. “Well do you want to stay with me Rex? If you stay that’s what I will call you.”

Rex and Daniel became almost inseparable.

One night while taking Rex out for a walk a cat came out of an alley saw Rex and ran off.

Rex suddenly chased after the cat. Daniel thought he would wait there. Rex will come back he thought. As he waited a man came up to him and said “give me your money or I will stick this knife into you.” Daniel was being robbed. Daniel said “I have no money on me.” The man got angry. “Everyone has money on them.”

“I left mine at home” said Daniel. The man said “I’m going to kill you”. Just then Rex came back and just grabbed the man’s arm. He dropped the knife and Rex was growling and let go of his arm. He stood in front of Daniel. The man just turned and ran away. You see Daniel had helped Rex back to health and Rex saw his master in trouble and helped him. If we are kind to animals this kind of human animal friendship would happen with all animals in time. So if you help any animal it will always remember you and recognize you if you meet again.

“It’s like today” said Grandpa. You and Manuel have a kind heart for all animals and they sense it and came to show you they can be kind and loving to those who love them lots of animals are like this. Mind you I don’t think I would go up to a lion and kiss it! It might not be too happy and think I’m its dinner! I wonder if you will see the wolves again.

“I hope we do Grandpa. I like them a lot and Manuel named his wolf Mr Wolf.” That’s nice Manuel. I expect you would like him to live with you!”

“Yes please he can sleep in our bedroom.” Grandpa smiled. “Time for bed you two”.

While Manuel was brushing his teeth grandpa asked me if Manuel was saying a lot more words now with me.” Oh yes I said. “He does and he also says quite a few words while he’s asleep.”

“He’s just dreaming Pedro” said Grandpa. “Yes but I don’t talk in my sleep.” “How do you know? You are asleep. Go on off to bed.

Goodnight you two" said Grandpa. "Goodnight grandpa." Manuel then said "thank you Mr Grandpa for looking after me." "It's a pleasure Manuel. Said Grandpa. "Well he seems to be finding his tongue at last. Sleep tight you two."

CHAPTER 8

Next morning everything seemed to be back to normal. Eggs on toast for breakfast and Grandpa sitting on the porch. "I must start on the vegetable plot, have a clear up and plant some more things said Grandpa. " Still it's nice to sit and watch the birds, butterflies and bees. They don't rush about. They just get on with things at a leisurely pace. Ah well there's no rush for planting. All next week untouched yet!"

"Pedro I've got to go and see Dr Rodriguez later. Will you stay around until I get back?" said Grandpa. "Yes I will. But why are you going to see him? Are you unwell? "Not really. Said Grandpa. "Just a little problem to get checked out. You know how to plant potato tubers don't you Pedro ?"

"Yes you showed me how". Well perhaps while I'm gone you could plant five rows out. Manuel will help. That will give me a good start on re-planting the vegetable garden".

"I've got to go now Pedro" said Grandpa. I won't be long".
"O.K. Grandpa. We will start on the potatoes."

Manuel and I had finished planting the potatoes and tidied up around the house. Grandpa had been gone for quite a while. Manuel asked why grandpa was not back. Just then grandpa came along the track towards the house. "Did you have a nice visit with Dr Rodriguez?   "Yes fine".

Grandpa didn't look himself even Manuel must have sensed something was not right. "Mr Grandpa is not happy" he said.

"We've put the potatoes in grandpa".
"Thanks Pedro. I'm just going to have a little rest. I have some thinking to do. You two can do what you want to do now".

"What shall we do Manuel?" I want to stay here. Mr Grandpa not well."

As Manuel seemed to have a knack for knowing when things aren't right we stayed do some chores to help grandpa out. "Perhaps he's tired out. He does most things for us and for the house and garden. Don't make too much noise Manuel so that grandpa can rest."

"No I won't. I will bang things softly." Said Manuel.

“You are funny Manuel and you are the best brother I had always wanted.”

“Is that good Pedro?

“Yes very good Manuel.”

We were just about to start on the chores when Dr Rodriguez came by. “Do you want grandpa?

“No it’s you and Manuel I want to talk to. You see your Grandpa has been feeling unwell and tired. I don’t suppose he said anything to you over the last few months.”

“No, Grandpa did not seem to be his normal self”

“What he needs is for you and Manuel to do a lot more chores so that he can get his strength back with rest. Do you understand Pedro?

“Yes I think so.”

“Don’t tell him I called. Just do as much as you can to help him.”

“I won’t tell him it’s our little secret.”

“Good that’s he best way. Are you okay Manuel?

"Yes thank you Mr Doctor."

"O.K. good I'll be off now"

"Goodbye Dr Rodriguez."

"Come on Manuel we had better make a list of things that we can help grandpa out with. Here's a piece of paper and pencil. 1. Milk Matilda, 2. Dig up potatoes said Manuel. "No Manuel, we have just put them in" I said. 3. Sweep up our room. 4. Get fire ready. 5. Go to village to get groceries. I think that's enough otherwise grandpa will have nothing to do and he won't want to get out of his chair. I'll make us a sandwich then after that we can start".

“Can I have a honey sandwich? Said Manuel.

“Yes if you like. Yuk that’s too sicky for me. I’ll have cheese”.

CHAPTER 9

A week went by and Manuel and I did lots of things to help Grandpa but he was not getting better. He just did a few things like getting breakfast for me and Manuel. Grandpa didn't seem to be eating very much of his breakfast. He just picked at it and pushes it aside

"Are you not hungry Grandpa? I said.

"I seem to have lost my appetite." Grandpa said.

“Is there anything we can get you to eat that you would like?”

“Yes, a few strawberries from the garden might be nice.”

“Oh good. Come on Manuel lets get grandpa some strawberries.”

We picked quite a few and gave them to grandpa. He picked up one and ate only half of it. “Sorry you two but I just don’t feel like eating anymore. You and Manuel finish them off. I’m going to sit on the porch.”

I was getting worried now that grandpa wasn't eating hardly any food at all. "Grandpa will you be o.k. for a while?"

"Yes of course. I'm not an invalid yet."

"We won't be long. Come on Manuel." "Where are we going? said Manuel.

"I will tell you in a minute. I don't want to worry grandpa"

On the way to the village I told Manuel that I was worried about grandpa. Then Manuel suddenly said "Mr Grandpa won't die will he"?

“No of course not. He is just tired.”

What Manuel had just said made me think what if grandpa did die. What would Manuel and I do? I must stop thinking of silly things. Grandpa will soon be fine with our help. We arrived at Dr Rodriguez house. His wife Maria said “Hello you two. Is this is a friendly visit?

“Well sort of. I’m worried about grandpa.”

“Come in. My husband is out on house call to visit a lady who will soon have a baby. He won’t be long. Would you like some milk and chocolate cake?” “Yes lots” said Manuel.

Maria laughed. "O.K. Manuel I will find you a big slice."

"He's much bigger than me Mrs Rodriguez so he needs more I suppose".

"Its lovely that you have taken Manuel into live with you".

"Oh he's part of our family now." "That's lovely. Cake coming up. Here you are Manuel a giant slice and a jug of milk." said Mrs Rodriguez.

"Wow if I eat lots I would burst." said Manuel.

“Here’s yours Pedro.”

Not quite as much thank you”.

Before we could finish our cake Dr Rodriguez came in. “Hello you two. How is your grandpa?

“He’s not eating very much food. In fact he ate hardly anything. Could you come by some time to see him and help him get his appetite back?

“I tell you what. I’m going fishing in the lake past your house. I will stop by and check your grandpa out and see what I can do. Don’t worry too much. It may be the tiredness. He will take a little longer to get better because of his age. I'll come by in a couple of hours."

"Thank you Dr Rodriguez. We had better get back to grandpa now to see if he wants anything." "Just a minute Pedro here's an apple pie for your grandpa. I know he likes that and for you two the rest of the chocolate cake." said Mrs Rodriguez. "Wow thank you". "Is that all mine? Said Manuel.

"No Manuel. Some for you and some for me." I said.

"Can I have the biggest for my piece?" "Yes okay. Come on lets get back." "Bye Pedro. Bye Manuel." said Mrs Rodriguez.

“Bye Mrs Rodriguez” we shouted.

It was so lovely on the way back. There were butterflies of all colours. Dragonflies flying all around. There was a lovely smell of flowers on the breeze. “We’re lucky Manuel to have nature all around us. I couldn’t live anywhere else.” I said.

“No me too. Will I see Mr Wolf soon”?

“He will come and see you again Manuel when he’s not so busy.”

“What does he do when he’s busy?”

“I don’t really know but I expect its something important Manuel. There’s Grandpa still in the chair.”

“Hello Grandpa. Did you miss us?

“I think so. I mean I must have dozed off. It’s like you just left.”

“I hope you don’t mind but we went to see Dr Rodriguez because we were worried that you won’t eat much.” I said.

“Bless you. I’ll be fine soon”.

“Dr Rodriguez said he would come by on his way to fishing in the lake.

“If I felt better I would like to go fishing too. “

“You will soon Grandpa. Here’s a home made apple pie for you. Mrs Rodriguez sent it.”

“I’ll take a slice later. That’s very kind of her. I like Mrs Rodriguez. She’s a good lady.”

“We like her too and her chocolate cake. She gave us the rest of the cake to take home.”

“That’s nice but don’t you two eat it all at once. Save some for later” said Grandpa.

"Okay grandpa."

"Manuel can you get some logs in and put them by the fire. I still feel the cold at night." said Grandpa.

"Come on Manuel. You pick up 5 logs and I will pick up one,   because you are much bigger than me. If we pick up two lots of logs that will do for tonight I think." I said.

It soon became evening. The fire was burning well. Grandpa was sitting in his chair. He looked deep in thought. Manuel and I sat on the floor close to the fire. The flames were giving a flickering light on the walls. We both kept quiet as grandpa needed to rest as much as possible. Manuel pointed to the side of the fireplace. “Look a mouse! “Oh it’s only Messy my pet mouse. He’s come to enjoy the warmth.”

Manuel gave me a little piece of chocolate cake. “Give it to Mousie he’s hungry.” I put the piece of cake next to Messy and he smelt it and started to gobble it down. He must have been hungry. After he had finished Manuel said “Look fat mouse!”

I looked at messy. He was sitting still and his tummy was looking big. “You’ve eaten too much!” We both laughed. Soon messy was asleep and so was Grandpa. It was funny to watch Messy. He was making a squeaky snore and grandpa was snoring like a hippo!

After a while Grandpa woke up. “Look at the time. Off to bed you two.” said Grandpa. “Messy is sleeping by the fireplace I said. “That’s o.k. leave him there. Where are your little lizards?”

“I haven’t seen them lately. In my bed when it’s cold.”

“Well goodnight you two.” “Goodnight Mr Grandpa.

I hope you feel better soon”.

“Thanks Manuel”

We went to bed. When I was ready I pulled back my blanket and to my surprise my little lizard friends were there. “It’s cold. Move over lizards. There’s plenty of room for us all. Manuel asked me where my lizards were. “I expect these two will tell their friends how nice it is in our beds and two more will come and sleep with you” I said “Oh good I can’t wait. Goodnight Manuel.” “Goodnight Pedro.”

The next day just as Grandpa was getting breakfast Dr Rodriguez came by. “You are early Dr” I said. “Yes I’ll fish up until midday. After that it’s too hot”

“Oh yes of course.” “How would you two like to go fishing you two? Said Dr Rodriguez.”

“Oh yes please.”

“Is that o.k. with you Joseph? Will you be alright for a few hours”?

“Yes fine. Just a minute I’ll make you two a sandwich each to eat on your way.” said Grandpa. “Thanks Grandpa. “Are you two ready?

“Yes Dr Rodriguez.” “Bye Joseph. We’ll be back by midday.”

"Bye Grandpa." Manuel just waved at grandpa because he had a mouth full of sandwich.

CHAPTER 10

When we got to the lake Dr Rodriguez got his fishing rod ready. He put a piece of cheese on the hook and cast it into the water. “I only have one rod so you can take it in turns to hold it and you might catch a fish.” After a while Dr Rodriguez said “Here Manuel you can hold the rod. It’s your turn.” “ Thank you.” No sooner was it in Manuel’s hand than the line tightened. “Turn the reel Manuel like this.” said the Dr.

There was such joy on Manuel’s face. He had never been fishing before. “Pull it in! Oh hard luck Manuel it's a bicycle wheel." "That's not a fish" said Manuel. "No Manuel but you caught something".

We didn't catch anything that morning. I was glad in a way because we would have had to take the fish away from its family. "I've had enough. Boy it's hot. Let's get back." Said the Dr. "O.K Dr Rodriguez. Can I carry your rod. ? "Yes of course Manuel. But be careful where you are pointing it."

When we arrived home I said to Dr Rodriguez "Grandpa is asleep in his chair again." "He needs all the rest he can get" said the Dr. Just then Grandpa's head fell forward onto his chest. “You boys go into the house. I’ll just check Joseph out.”

From the kitchen I heard Dr Rodriguez say “oh dear”. “Stay here Manuel. I will ask Dr Rodriguez how grandpa is.” “ How is Grandpa?

“Ah, Pedro. Sit down on the bench there. There is no easy way to tell you this. Your grandpa has passed away. It looks as if it was peaceful. I think his body was worn out. I’m sorry Pedro.”

I was shocked. I couldn’t move. “He’s just sleeping he’s not dead.”

"I'm afraid he is dead Pedro" said the Dr. Manuel came out. "Mr Grandpa dead like Sophia." "Yes Manuel he is."

Manuel sat by me and put his arm around me. The shock turned to grief and we both started crying. Dr Rodriguez put a sheet over Grandpa. It was so strange. Grandpa was alive this morning and now he's dead. Dr Rodriguez put his arms around us. "You will come and stay with Maria and me until we can sort things out." said Dr Rodriguez. "No I want to stay here. We have to look after Matilda and the other animals" I said.

It was all so sudden. We couldn't take it in. it was like a bad dream.

“Just come home with me until I can get your grandpa laid to rest. Later today you can come home. I know you are a very sensible boy and Manuel will be of comfort to you.”

It still felt like a dream. We walked away from the house. I held Manuel’s hand. He was not saying anything. His face was a blank. It seemed ages to get to Dr Rodriguez’ house.

I heard Mrs Rodriguez crying. She came out and sat between us. “I’m so sorry” she said.

“What will happen to us?” I said. “Don’t worry we will sort it all out. Just stay tonight with us.”

“No thanks we have to feed the animals and take care of them and tidy up. Grandpa wouldn’t like it if we stopped looking after things.”

“Okay Pedro look after Manuel but if you get lonely please come back here. You are most welcome. Have you food at home?

“Yes plenty thank you. We have fruit, cheese and bread. That’s all we need.”

“Okay. I’ll tell Dr Rodriguez you’ve gone.”

CHAPTER 11

Manuel and I walked home. We never said a word on the way back. As we arrived home I saw Matilda and Messy. Matilda was lying down and Messy was lying against her. I had never seen that before. They also looked like two orphans. When we went into the house it was very strange grandpa was gone but not gone. His presence was still felt in the house. It's hard to explain. Its something you feel. Manuel said "we will live here forever." Yes it's our home and we have our fellow creatures to look after." I said.

That night we just picked at our food. Even my little mouse friend Messy wouldn't eat the piece of cheese I put down. Grandpa didn't really approve of me feeding messy but a couple of times I saw him put some bits of cheese down for messy to eat. He was just a softee really.

We were all feeling very tired. It had been a very sad day and we still couldn't take it in. we went to bed early. I woke up the next day before Manuel and went out into the kitchen expecting to see Grandpa and thinking maybe it had all been a bad dream. But the house was silent. Manuel must have been tired out. Most mornings I would come out and see Grandpa working in the garden. He liked to work early in the day while it was still cool. All I could see was his garden fork still in the soil where he left it. I suddenly wondered how we were going to get money to buy things then I remembered Grandpa said that if he had to go into hospital or away from the house for a while there was some money he had saved up in a jar under the kitchen sink. I looked and found the jar. It had 200 euros in it. Not a fortune but it took Grandpa a long time to save it up in case of an emergency. Still if we were careful and eat our fruit and vegetables from the garden the money might last a long time.

I heard Manuel getting up. He came into the kitchen a bit drowsy.

“Would you like some breakfast Manuel?

“Yes please I feel very hungry” said Manuel.

“It’s not surprising. We didn’t eat hardly anything yesterday”.

There was some bread from yesterday and a little cheese and two slices of ham. We finished it all. Our tummies were still rumbling after we had eaten. “We will have to buy some food Manuel. We will go to the village later” I said.

After tidying up and feeding the animals we both sat down on the porch. I think we were both feeling a little lost. Everything happened so quickly.

“Hello Pedro and Manuel”. It was Dr Rodriguez with the Mayor, Mr Garcia. “We have been having a chat about your futures.” said Dr Rodriguez.

“That’s okay we will be fine here.” I said.

“I’m sorry Pedro but you can’t stay here on your own. You are too young and have no job or money.

“Yes we have Mr Mayor. We have 200 euros.”

“That will only last a few weeks. Then what? No Pedro it will not work and Manuel needs special care. “I can do that” I said.

“No I’m sorry but he will have to go to a special centre for adults with learning problems in Madrid.”

“No that’s cruel he would hate it. No friends or animals”!

“That’s the only solution Pedro. Dr Rodriguez and Maria will look after you until we can sort things out for you. I will get Maria to start to make you up a room. Don’t worry we will do all we can for you.”

“But can’t Manuel come too”? “No. Sorry he needs special care”. Said Dr Rodriguez.

I looked at Manuel who was smiling. He doesn’t know what’s going to happen I thought. Then in my mind I had an idea. I would agree to all the things they said as long as we can stay here one more night to put things straight and make the house safe but the next time they come back to get us we will be gone. I'm not leaving Manuel or Matilda or Piggy or Messy. We will all live together far away where no one can find us.

"Dr Rodriguez I think you and Mr Garcia are right. I wouldn't know what to do if I ran out of money and Manuel needs special care as you said."

"There's a good boy Pedro, you see when you think about it, it's best for both of you. "

"I would like just one more night at Grandpa's before everything changes and

Manuel has to go into care." I said. "Why not? One more night wont matter if that's okay with you Mr Garcia."

"Yes I suppose so. If it settles your mind Pedro."

"Thank you Mr Garcia."

"Have you enough food for tonight? said Mr Garcia.

"Yes we have plenty."

"Don't worry we will find your animals good homes. Right Pedro we will be over about

10.am tomorrow morning. Make sure you are ready."

"Yes we will thank you. "

"Goodbye and see you in the morning. Said Dr Rodriguez. "Come on Mr Garcia come home with me. I have some great wine for you to try. "That's an offer I can't refuse Dr Rodriguez."

CHAPTER 12

When Dr Rodriguez and Mr Garcia were out of sight I started to prepare our escape. "Manuel, I know you don't really understand what's going on but they want to separate us and put you into a special home. Do you want to? “No I want to stay with you here.” said Manuel.

“If we stay here Manuel they will come tomorrow and put us in care. I think you understand a bit more than I thought. Let’s get our things together and go away so that can’t put us in care. We will need food and some money. Some clothes, matches and that old tent in the shed. It’s not very big but big enough for us and don’t forget our photos of Grandpa and Sophia. I nearly forgot! What about Matilda, Piggy and Messy. They are our family as well so they can come with us. Dr Rodriguez said they would find good homes for them but I would be always wondering if they were o.k. We had better get going soon. It’s only a few hours until dark”

We both packed everything up quickly. Manuel took the big pack on his back with lots of food and tins of cat food. Grandpa always kept a lot in the cupboard. “Matilda is okay. She eats grass and stuff. Are you ready Manuel? “Yes Pedro.”

“Where is Messy? Oh there you are, on the sideboard. I will put you in my top pocket. You will be safe and warm. Come on. Let’s go. We can camp when we are well away from here for the night”

I locked the front door and said to the house. “We will be back one day. If your spirit is watching over us Grandpa I worry we will be fine and you could come along and see we are safe.”

“Where is Grandpa Pedro? “

“Well he’s not here but his goodness will protect us.” I said.

We all took one last look at the house that had been a place of love and kindness. What was strange is that Matilda and Piggy seemed to understand. It was strange. We set off over the hill behind the house. We walked for about 3 hours. It was getting dark.

"Let's camp here by these rocks. It's sheltered".

Manuel took off the big pack off his back and we laid out two small blankets. "We can sleep under the stars tonight. It's lovely and warm".

We had some bread and cheese and some biscuits. I gave piggy her cat food. We had no plates so I just put it on the flat rock. "Messy here is some cheese for you. "

Matilda was okay she just grazed on the grasses around us. Manuel and I had a good supper. I lit a small fire with some old dead tree branches. It was really wonderful. We were all together. Us against the world and its silly rules and regulations. We just wanted to be left in peace to be happy.

“Its bedtime Manuel.”

“I’m really tired Pedro. “

We lay down and pulled the blankets over us. Piggy laid by my side. Messy slept by my head and Matilda slept by the rocks. “Goodnight Manuel.” “Goodnight Pedro and sleep tight everyone.”

I was woken up the next morning by birds singing. It was quite loud. I felt so happy we were one family. A bit odd maybe, but still a family and probably happier than millions of families around the world.

“I’m hungry Pedro.” said Manuel

“O.k. good morning Manuel. Did you sleep well?

“Not too bad. It was Matilda who woke me up with her snoring. I think she ate too much rich grass. Hello piggy. Hello messy. I hope you slept well.”

“We will all sleep better when we get used to our outdoor life and when we have had breakfast. We must carry on further away from our village and the nasty people who want to put us in care. We don't need that. We can take care of ourselves." I said.

Our breakfast was our usual meal of biscuits and cheese. "We have run out of bread Manuel. We will stop at the next village and get some food. We can fill up our water bottles from the mountain stream later."

As we walked to the village I said to Manuel. "You stay here and look after our little family. It's best if I go into the village alone. It will be less curious for the people." "Okay I stay Pedro and wait for you."

It was a very small village. About seven houses with old people just sitting on chairs shading from the sun. The first old lady I saw smiled and said. "Where are your family? You are young to be out here in the wilds by yourself. "

"They are just over the hill resting so I came to see if you could sell us some bread. We are on a nature walk." I said.

"There are wolves in the mountains; so take care young man. What is your name?" "I am Pedro."

"I am Nora. Our village is dying because no young people want to live out this far. I have some bread I baked this morning. You are lucky I made so much you can have two loaves." "Thank you, Nora. How much do I owe you? "

"Nothing. "If I can help someone who is in need then I am happy. I have some spare goat's cheese. Would you like some of that? Said Nora.

"Thank you. You are very kind."

"We see very few strangers out here. It is lovely to have the company of someone new. All of the villagers are over 80 years old. "

"Where are your family? I asked.

"They left home to work in the big city many years ago. They come home once a year to see me "explained Nora.

"That's awful. They should come much more." I said.

"I've given up worrying about it. They are too busy with their jobs, big houses and motor cars to even think about me. "

"I must go now Nora. I will never forget your kindness and I will think about you a lot."

"That's made my heart glad Pedro and brought a tear to my eye."

“Goodbye Nora.”

“Take care Pedro and give my love to your family.”

As I walked away it made me feel very sad. We could have stayed and helped the old villagers but we had to keep out in the wilds so we didn’t get caught.

“Hello Manuel. “

“Hello Pedro I thought you were lost. We are glad to see you. Did you get some food”?

“Yes, lovely fresh bread with - yes you’ve guessed it cheese! I think we will turn into mice. There was a lovely old lady in the village. So kind to a stranger. One day I will make her very happy. I just know I will one day. Lets all go to that valley over there and settle down to rest and stay the night. This place looks nice. It's green with flowers waving in the breeze. Where is messy?

"She's in my bag. She got tired so I carried her." Piggy and Matilda lay down with each other.

"Look there's a stream. Lets all go for a drink. The mountain water is so cool and sweet" I said.

We settled down for our supper. The bread was very tasty and so was the goat's cheese. Messy liked the cheese and Piggy had a tin of cat food.

"Not much cat food left Manuel."

"Can't we buy some at the next shop?

"There are no shops in the mountains Manuel. We will manage though. Piggy will just have to learn to like bread and cheese. We also sometimes find berries and nuts on trees and some wild fruit trees with lovely pears. Matilda is happy she can eat anything; that's what goats do."

As it grew dark we laid down to look at the stars.

“How many stars are there Pedro.”

“Grandpa used to say there were billions of stars”.

“What’s a billion Pedro”?

“Oh a bit less than a squillion I think. They say if you join up the stars in the sky you can make figures or animals. Some people can tell your fortune by a star sign. Grandpa used to say its mumbo jumbo. Shall we all go to bed now? “Goodnight Manuel. Goodnight Messy. Goodnight Piggy, goodnight Matilda.

“Its just as well there’s not 50 of us. It would take all night to say goodnight !

CHAPTER 13

The next day we woke up. “Hello everyone did you all sleep well”? I said.

“Yes Pedro” said Manuel “I expect the animals said yes in their own way! “Where’s Matilda?

“She’s over there Pedro in that ditch.”

“Come out Matilda we’ve got to get some breakfast and then move on” I said. But Matilda would not leave the ditch so I went over to get her and to my surprise in the ditch next to a big sheep was a little lamb. The sheep was lying on one side and not moving. I touched her but she was cold and had died. The little lamb must be so hungry. “But we have no milk.” I said. “Yes we do Pedro. Matilda used to give milk.”

“Oh yes of course. Good thought Manuel! I had forgotten about that and all this time we could have had some of Matilda’s milk with our food “

We put the lamb next to Matilda. She must have sensed the little lamb was so hungry and let the lamb get some milk from her udders. “Look Manuel. The lamb is having a feast and Matilda just lets the lamb have all it wants. We will have to take the sweet lamb with us. It won’t survive on its own. We will adopt it.” “But what shall we call her Pedro? She’s lucky we found her. “

“That’s it we will call her Lucky “I said.

“I hope we don’t meet an elephant.” said Manuel. I don’t think we could cope with that.”

“There are no elephants in Spain” I said.

After breakfast we set off again. “Is everyone here?”

“There are Piggy, Messy, Matilda and Lucky.” said Manuel.

“Come on then. Let’s see what’s over the next hill. It’s quite a way it will take us all morning to get there I expect.” “You are quiet Manuel. Are you okay”?

“Yes Pedro. I’m so happy we have a big family now. I like to take care of them and that makes me feel calm. I’ve never been so happy in all my life.”

"Ah that's lovely Manuel. We are the six Musketeers - All for one and one for all!"

It took us about 3 hours to reach the hill. "I've never been this far before. It's getting more remote. Look Manuel over there! Lovely meadows and wild flowers and there's an old ruined house and barn by the trees. Let's explore." I wondered if this could this be our new home together. We were all tired and wanted to rest so we went to explore the old ruin.

Although it was run down the roof was still good and with a bit of tidying it might suit us. As we looked out of the back of the house we could see lots of fruit trees; fig trees and grape vines.

"We can live well here except poor old Piggy's cat food doesn't grow on trees". Just then piggy run up a fig tree and started to eat some figs. I remember now grandpa used to say she liked figs and sometimes a little fruit. It looked like we had found our new home.

"I'm sure I could go back to the old village once a week to buy bread from the old lady or other villagers and if I go on my own I can make it much faster there and back. But we are okay for now.

There is your own lovely meadow Matilda for you to graze on and give Lucky lots of milk. Messy likes fruit and berries and there's an old well for water. Drop a stone down it Manuel; let's hear if there is water down there. "

"Okay. We heard a splash. "Oh good water Pedro!

"Can we eat now Pedro I'm very hungry?"

"Okay. We still have bread and cheese left and now lots of fruit, berries and some almonds ".

Matilda was grazing and Lucky was having some of her milk. Piggy was still up in the fig tree and Messy was eating berries. “Its great here and we have food Manuel. When we have eaten and rested lets tidy up the house so we can settle down. We have a few hours till night time. “

After a while Manuel and I started to clean the house. There was an old broom in the cupboard so Manuel brushed hard and made lots of dust. There were some old tables and chairs that needed fixing and other things like old pots which would be useful. “Look Manuel our family is so tired they are all sleeping together. Matilda is lying down with all the animals. We are free of people who think they know what’s best for us. Why don’t they stop trying to make us unhappy and put us in an institution or an orphanage? Grandpa used to say the world is full of “do gooders” many good but many bad.

The sun was going down and we were so tired. Manuel and I lay down on some old straw and fell asleep. I woke first and looked out at our new home. It was wonderful. To most people it would look run down and dirty but to us it was paradise.

“Hello Pedro”

“Good morning Manuel. Did you sleep well?”

“Yes better today thank you. “

“You needed a good rest as we all did. I will go to the well and pull up a bucket of water. We can wash ourselves. Our animal family wash and lick them selves clean! I will fill that tin bowl full of water for our family to drink.”

“Can we stay here forever Pedro?”

“I hope so Manuel”.

It was hard work pulling up the bucket from the well so I asked Manuel to help. He is so strong he pulled up buckets of water so easily. “It’s nice how we all help each other. Wouldn’t the world be a wonderful place if everyone helped each other with kindness and everyone had food and shelter like us? I will have to go back to the old village because we are out of bread and cheese Manuel. I will go soon so I can get back not too late. I will try to be as quick as I can. Look after everyone Manuel”.

“Okay Pedro.”

The way back to the village seemed ages but it was probably about 2 hours. As I entered the village Nora was in her rocking chair on her veranda. She gave me a big smile when she saw me.

“Pedro I thought you had gone miles away for good.”

“No, not too far away” Some other village folk came to say hello. “Nora has told us about you. “Have you come for a visit?”

“Yes and to buy some supplies if you can sell me some”

“What would you like Pedro? Some of my bread and goats cheese?

“Yes please Nora.”

“I have a couple of jars of honey said one villager” And another said I could have some eggs.

“Thank you very much. What do I owe you?

“Don’t worry we can spare these few things.”

“You are so kind. Have you had any other visitors to your village?

“Yes Pedro. A travelling man with a monkey on a chain. He was very grumpy because we didn’t give him some honey when he made the sweet little monkey do some tricks. The poor monkey didn’t look happy.

“Has the man gone far”?

“One of the villagers saw him just over that ridge. He’s camping there.”

I stayed and chatted to Nora and the villagers for a while. “I had better start back now. Thank you all so much for your kindness. “

They put the food in a bag for me and I waved goodbye. “Come back again Pedro.”

“I will if I can.”

On my way out to the open countryside I thought of the poor monkey so I went over towards the ridge and there tied to a tree on a chain was the little monkey. The man was asleep with an empty bottle on the ground. He had had too much to drink and was sleeping it off. The monkey saw me and put its hands out like a greeting. I crept up to it and unchained it. “Keep quiet monkey. Come and live with our family. You will be loved and cared for.”

The little monkey climbed onto my shoulder and we quietly crept away. After we got far enough away I stopped and the monkey jumped down and ran to a tree with some sort of fruit on it. He ate lots. He was very hungry. “Come on lets get home to our family far away from that evil man. Someone should put him on a chain and make him do tricks." I said.

It took about another hour to get home. I was getting tired. What with carrying the bag of food and the monkey on my shoulder. Manuel saw me.

"I am glad you are back Pedro. What's that another one for our family"?

The monkey jumped from me onto Manuel's shoulders. "I like him said Manuel with a big smile."

"It looks like he has a new friend. Let's see what the others make of him. I don't know if it's a boy or a girl. Well it doesn't matter."

Matilda come over and sniffed the monkey then the lamb Piggy and Messy came to see the new arrival. As the monkey sat on the ground all the animals licked him like saying welcome to your new family it was so nice to see.

"What shall we call him or her? What about peanut. That's a monkey name."

"I like that Pedro."

“Good. Peanut it is. Lets all have a feast. I have some nice food from the kind villagers. We can have honey on bread or our usual cheese. What shall we have”?

“Honey please Pedro. “

Manuel suddenly looked a bit sad. “I remember my mummy Sophia used to give me honey on crusty bread as a treat. I will think of her when I eat it. She was lovely to me. Will I see her again Pedro. ?

“Yes in heaven one day. “

“Now I am happy again Pedro.”

“This is nice sweet honey and bread” said Manuel. We both enjoyed a feast. After we all had our different foods we went to the trees at the side of the meadow. There was a nice breeze which kept us cool. Peanut, Matilda, Lucky, Messy and Piggy lay down to enjoy a cool rest.

“Our family is getting bigger but it’s lovely to be at one with nature. In a fast world of greed and possessions I think here is paradise. We have our family. That gives Manuel and me so much pleasure and fun and simple foods. Our life is so calm and uncomplicated. I think a lot of people would love to join us but I don’t think we would have enough bread and cheese to go around.”

While some of our family were having a snooze I was laying amongst the meadow flowers listening to the bees buzzing around. Crickets were chirruping. Swallows were diving up and down in the sky and a butterfly landed on my nose. It tickled. “Hello Mr butterfly I hope my nose is comfortable. Stay as long as you like.” It was a beautiful blue colour. I tried not to sneeze but it was tickling my nose so much! Attishoo ! It flew off. “Sorry Mr butterfly. Come back whenever you want and I’ll try not to sneeze next time! “

I could hear Manuel loudly snoring it sounded so loud he woke up the rest of our family. It had been a wonderful day. I hoped we would have millions more days like this with each other.

CHAPTER 14

I made many trips back to the village to get some food over the following weeks. Everything seemed idyllic. It was lovely to see the village folk. They always made me feel so welcome. I think they would love it if we all came to live with them. On the way back to our home I would often stop at a place where a stream was running in a valley. The mountain water was so sweet and cool to drink. I would lay down in a grassy meadow and look up at the clouds. Sometimes clouds took the shape of things. I would see things like dogs or peoples faces. I once thought I saw Grandpa. That was so lovely. Then the cloud vanished. When I got back near to our home our animal family would be waiting all together looking up the dusty track. They must have sensed I was nearly home.

“Hello I’m back again” I shouted. They would run to greet me. Messy always climbed onto Piggy’s back for a ride because she couldn’t run fast. It was so funny to see a mouse riding on a cat’s back. Peanut tried to get on Matilda’s back but she ran too fast for him to get on. We all had a cuddle and lucky licked my face. Her whiskers tickled. Piggy had become a vegetarian cat as we could no longer get tins of cat food. She likes figs, grapes and pears which is good because we have our old orchard full of many fruits and nuts; so with bread, cheese and fruit and nuts we all eat well. Matilda eats many green plants and I try the ones she eats and some are nice and some are bitter but I haven't had a tummy ache yet.

"Where's Manuel Peanut"? I said. He held my hand and took me to the barn and there was Manuel. He was fast asleep in the straw. "Let's not wake him Peanut. He must be tired.

"Let's go into the house." I said. It was a very hot day and much cooler indoors. Our animal family were glad to get out of the heat. Just then Manuel came in. “Pedro I have got a tummy ache.”

“How did you get it? Have you been eating too many figs while I was away.”?

“Yes I was hungry and couldn’t stop eating them.”

“Never mind that will soon go away. I often used to get tummy ache at grandpas when I ate too many unripe grapes. Lets all have a rest - it’s been a busy day”. What’s that Manuel outside? It sounds like a donkey noise”.

Manuel went to look. “Pedro there’s a lady on a donkey.”

I went to see. It was Nora from the village riding a donkey.

“Hello Pedro. Are these your family?”

“Yes but how did you find me?”

“Well there are only a few old houses out this far so I tried two and this one was the only one left. So I’m glad I’ve found you. Some policeman and a government official came to the village asking if we had seen two boys. One young boy and one older. We guessed that they wanted you and told us why and they wanted to take you back to a home and the older boy to an institution. I knew by the way you were so happy out in the woods that you would not want to go with them. Is that right?"

"Yes Nora. We are all so happy together they have no right to stop our happiness and the way we want to live."

"Can you all manage?" said Nora. "My father used to tell me of a very remote valley about 30 kilometres from here. He only went there once but said it was lovely and had a feeling of peace and joy. He also said he thought he saw a pure white figure of a man sitting by a large rock but when he went towards the rock the figure vanished. It could have been the bright sun shining on the rock but he never forgot how peaceful he felt the nearer he got to the rock. I will go back soon after I have rested just in case they come back and ask more questions. I told the other villagers to keep quiet to help you. They are all happy to say they know nothing."

"Here Nora, some of Matilda's milk - that will quench your thirst." Said Pedro.

"That's lovely Pedro. So rich and creamy. I love your animal family and Manuel"

Just then Peanut came over to Nora and sat by her and put his little hand on her arm. "Thank you sweet little one" she said and kissed peanut on the head. Then Messy, Matilda, Lucky and Piggy came to see Nora and sat around her. They sensed she was a caring person.

"I would love to come with you all but I'm too old to climb rocks and hills and the valley is too far for my old bones. I had better go now my lovely ones so I can get back before dark."

Manuel helped Nora onto the sweet little donkey. So Nora went off to the village. We waved her goodbye. "I hope I can see you all again one day" she said. "I know you will Nora; I just know you will." I said.

CHAPTER 15

As she got further away down the rough road we waved to her in the distance one more time. “Well Manuel it looks as though we will have to leave here soon and get far away from the police and people who are after us so they will never find us and we can settle down forever.

“Do we have to move Pedro?”

“I’m sorry Manuel but we have to. Let’s get a good night’s sleep and we can set of tomorrow”.

Matilda, Lucky, Piggy, Messy and Peanut came into the old house and settled down with us for the night. The next morning it was warm and sunny as usual. “We really need to take as much food with us as we can in case we don’t find any on the journey and I’ve an idea Manuel. There’s an old wooden cart in the barn. It looks strong and we can load it up with fruit, nuts and berries and put our things in it as well. Do you think you could pull it Manuel?"

"Yes easily Pedro. " We watched Manuel pull the cart out and bring it to the house. Being so strong he pulled it like a pram. "Let's load up with as much as we can get on it. Messy can sit on it. He will never walk a long way with us."

It must have taken a couple of hours to load up but at last we were ready. "Goodbye old house. Thank you for having us. I hope you get a new owner who will repair all your broken bits. Let's go everyone".

We took the dusty track north it was a hot day but there was a cool breeze which was nice. After a while Peanut picked up Messy who had fallen off the cart and jumped onto it with Messy.

Matilda, Lucky and Piggy trotted along behind the cart.

“All seems okay. How are you Manuel? Do you want a rest?

“No Pedro I can pull this all day.”

“We will stop around midday” I said.

The track went on and on. "What's the time Pedro"? Said Manuel.

I searched all my pockets but no watch. "I must have lost it or left it at the house. Still we don't need one anyway. What time it is doesn't matter to us anymore. We can roughly tell by the sun anyway. Grandpa showed me how to when I was 5 years old."

After a few miles the sun was right above us. "Let's stop soon Manuel. It's about midday and we need to find water and some shelter from the hot sun. Look there are a few trees by the stream over there. It must be the same stream that we passed many times. I wonder where the water comes from. Maybe it comes from the top of the mountain."

We had travelled about 4 kilometres from the old house and we were ready for a rest. Nobody seemed hungry but we all had a good drink from the little stream. Messy only had a little drink and sat in a shallow part cooling off. Soon all of us sat in the stream. It was lovely and cool. Manuel took off his shoes and soaked his feet in the stream.

"Let's all have a nap and wait until the midday sun passes over." I said.

As I lay down and rested a horrible thought came into my mind. What if they caught up with us and split up our family. No, no, no. It's not going to happen. Why do older people think they know what's best for us. Can't they just leave us in peace and get on with their own boring lives.

At school we used to get visiting inspectors from the schools department they were so sour faced like they had eaten lemons. They must have had a miserable childhood to look so grumpy. Even our teacher, Miss Garcia said when they left "I'm glad to see the back of those officials."

I must have dropped off to sleep because the next thing I remember was waking up with Peanut, Lucky and Matilda next to me.

“Are you ready to carry on Manuel”?

“Yes I’m ready Pedro.”

Everyone seemed okay after a rest.

“Where are Piggy and Messy, Manuel? “

“Over there by those rocks Pedro”.

“Come on you two we are going. Let’s get a few more hours walking in before we camp for the night. “

As we walked along the track it seemed as if we were the last people on earth. We were high up on the track and could see for miles across the countryside and could not see a house or farm anywhere in the distance. "This is great Manuel. We are getting far away from nasty people"

We were getting into remote countryside and there were less trees and flowers about. It was getting dusty and dessert like and the sun was still hot as we came to a bend in the track. I looked over towards an old tree standing on its own. Then a man in white with the most loving smile waved to me and pointed his hand towards some distant mountains. I turned to Manuel. "Look at that man by the tree." "What man Pedro?"

As I turned back to look he was gone. “The heat is making me see things that are not there. Let’s find a place to camp for the night. We are all tired.”

Manuel was pulling the cart with our few food supplies on it and Peanut, Lucky, Messy and Piggy were riding on it but Matilda was walking along beside Manuel.

“I’m tired Pedro and my muscles ache.”

“There’s a cave over there. We can get out of the sun and rest for the night”. As we got closer to the cave I felt a sense of unease. It was a big cave and anything could be in there. We were low on water and only had about enough for one more day. The water container on the cart was nearly empty and our food container was getting low. We hadn't seen any streams in this dusty dry place. "Let's just have a meal with what we have left and hope we find some food and supplies tomorrow."

We all shared the bread, fruit and dates and a small piece of cheese. Even Matilda who mostly eats grass was eating some bread and cheese as there was no grass about. It was getting dark. We were all so tired we must have just fallen asleep.

CHAPTER 16

The next day I woke up with Lucky, Peanut, Messy and Piggy lying next to me. It gets cold at night and they must have got close for warmth. I looked over towards where Manuel was sleeping and there by his side was a big wolf! Now what do
I do? The wolf just looked at me straight in the eyes.

It wasn't a threatening stare but one like a nice dog would give. Just then Manuel woke up.

"Good morning Mr Wolf" he said. I was still scared and Manuel could see I was. "Don't worry Pedro. This is nice Mr Wolf. He came to me last night and we slept together. He is all on his own and must have lost his pack. I told him he can come along with us."

"Will he let me stroke him? I said.

"Of course Pedro." He's nice.

"Well I suppose you are right Manuel. I slowly went over to the wolf and put my hand out to touch him. He then gave my hand a big wet lick with his tongue. Wow how fantastic. A nice kind wolf. You can come along with us if you like Mr Wolf."

He got up and went over to Matilda who would normally be a meal for a wolf but he just gave her a lick on her face. He also did the same to Piggy, Lucky and Peanut. They didn't seem frightened of him. They must have sensed he was a good wolf. He then looked down on Messy our little mouse. I picked up Messy and Mr Wolf gave her a big lick. Being so small his watery lick made her all wet but she was not bothered by this and climbed on his back. He turned his head and gave her nice friendly look.

"Welcome to our family Mr Wolf". I'm probably a bit daft but I think he understood me. We only had enough food now for a small breakfast. Then it was all gone. We had to get some more food and water soon. It was only early but it was getting hot already so we started off again. Everywhere was so barren. No trees grass or flowers just a few cactus trees like the prickly pear trees we had near our house which had fruit on them but out here there was no fruit. I was getting worried about what would happen if we found no food and water. We had been walking for a while but it was too hot.

“Let’s rest again Manuel. I suppose there’s no point in you pulling the cart along as its empty.”

“Better keep it Pedro in case we find some food to put on it.”

"Good idea Manuel I hope you are right. We need food soon."

There was no sign of life or villages about. We really were far out in the wilds. We all sat down behind a large mound. It was shady from the sun. It was then that I remembered my grandfathers' words "never give up in finding your dream."

I hope so grandpa. I thought. But it all looks bleak at the moment.

"Pedro look!" Manuel was at the other side of the mound so I walked round to se what he was pointing at and to my shock and surprise our cart was full up with food. Fruit, nuts, bread, cheese and the water jugs were also full.

“I must be dreaming Manuel” “No its real Pedro look I’m eating an apple”

There were big baskets full of lovely food enough for a week or more. Just then Mr Wolf came over.

“I hope you like bread and fruit that’s all we have.” I said.

He took an apple from the basket and ate it. “Oh good you’re a vegetarian Mr wolf”

I wondered where all this lovely food came from. My grandpa used to say we all have a guardian angel. Perhaps we had one helping us. As I looked back to the others there was the man all in white standing on the mound. I rubbed my eyes to make sure I wasn't seeing things and yes he was still there. He gave me a smile and waved to me and then vanished. The food was real so the man must be. It was all very strange but I felt so happy for all of us. We could now go on to find our dream place of peace altogether.

"I hope we get to meet that nice kind man. "How did he just vanish though?" He must be our guardian angel. How lovely to think that he may be. Come on everyone lets have a feast before we move on."

"I'm starving Pedro. I don't know what to eat first" exclaimed Manuel.

"Well how about some bread, cheese, nuts and an apple or two."

"Yes lovely Pedro. "

We all had some goodies. Manuel and I had some lovely crusty bread with cheese. Peanut had lots of nuts and dried fruit to eat. Messy had some cheese, Piggy had dried fruit and cheese, Matilda had some apples and bread and Lucky had Matilda's milk. We all felt full up but we had to move on again soon.

CHAPTER 17

We packed up the cart and Manuel started to pull the cart up the track. Messy got a ride on Mr Wolf's back again. Piggy and Peanut sat on the cart and Matilda and Lucky trotted along. We must have covered about 5 kilometres. Everyone looked happy. Well you can't really tell with Mr Wolf because he doesn't smile much.

Suddenly a short way in front of us the man in white appeared. He said in a soft voice. “You will soon be home just a little further” then he vanished. What did he mean? I wondered. “We will be soon be home” There was nothing but rocks and barren land around but he had been so good to us we had to trust him. He was our best hope out of here in the wilds.

“Can you pull the cart anymore today Manuel?

“Yes of course I’m not tired”. He said.

Everyone looked o.k. "Let's carry on to that valley. It doesn't look too far away"

After probably about a couple of kilometres we came into the valley which was rocky and dusty like everywhere in the wilds.

"Oh dear I hope this isn't the home our guardian angel was talking about. Let's rest everyone."

We were all a bit tired and the sun was very hot. We found a place away from the sun's heat. We must have all fallen asleep. I don't know how long we were all sleeping but I was suddenly woken up by Manuel.

“Look Pedro. Grass, trees flowers and water”.

I rubbed my eyes. “It must be a mirage. Is it real ? Pedro was eating an apple from the tree. There were so many trees in the valley where before there were none. Just then a voice said “just a bit further to your home of dreams.”

We could not see anyone but we all went to look around this beautiful, lush green valley.

There were fruit trees of every kind. Huge flowers everywhere with lovely scent. Cool clear streams of water, butterflies, birds singing and little animals everywhere. It was like a book I read once about a place called paradise or an oasis in the wilderness. It was real though "so enjoy it everyone" I said.

Peanut climbed up the trees picking fruit. Piggy and Messy had two big butterflies on their backs. It looked so funny. Manuel was going from tree to tree eating as much fruit as he could.

"Take it easy Manuel you will get tummy ache" I said.

"Okay. Pedro I like it here can we stay?"

"Yes of course".

Matilda and Lucky had so much green grass to eat and Mr Wolf just lay down and watched us. I don't know what he was thinking but he looked content. I knew now what the man in white meant when he said "just a little further to your home of dreams". This must be it surely. As I looked back beyond the valley it was barren and dusty and yet here it was so wonderful.

CHAPTER 18

Several days went past. We did not see the man in white but explored the valley. Living here was like the most beautiful dream anyone could have. All the animals in the valley were small and so friendly. Piggy, Messy, Lucky and Peanut also found new friends. Messy had lots of mice to play with and Piggy who used to chase birds now just sat and watched them fly. So many birds and colours and lovely birdsong.

Lucky seemed to like having butterflies land on her and taking them for a ride. Peanut found some baby monkeys so cute and small with lovely golden colour fur. He liked to chase them up the trees and have fun. Manuel and Matilda went off to explore. I expect they will have a lovely time with new animal friends. It gives me so much joy to see them so happy and content at last.

Time had no meaning here. We didn't have to worry about this and that at a certain time or eating at a certain time or going to school at a certain time. How lovely life was without the stress of time ! Everyone should trust in one way or another then people would realise they could control time not time control them and everyone's lives would be so much better.

"Hi Manuel. Did you and Matilda have fun?

"I talked to some big flowers; they were so nice and friendly we had a lovely chat!"

"You mean you talked to the flowers. They can't talk to you."

"Yes they can. Can't they Matilda?

Matilda bleated out a yes I think!

“Come with us past those trees. Quickly. Come on” shouted Manuel.

I went with Manuel. Matilda decided to stop and eat some grass. As we got past the trees there were hundreds of very big flowers all colours of the rainbow. Manuel said “I’m back flowers. Say hello to Pedro”.

I thought Manuel had a touch of too much sun heat. Then to my shock all the flowers said “hello Pedro, Manuel told us all about you. He says you are his best friend and we’ve met all your animal friends. Your monkey Peanut tried to pick a flower but we all told him off. That's not allowed we all live in harmony in the valley and all the animals plants and trees and flowers love each other and help each other."

"That's so nice Mr or Mrs Flower but how can you talk; you are just a flower?

"The nice man in white who made us all decided to give us a voice so we can talk to him."

"Do the other animals in the valley have voices to talk?" I asked.

"Of course!   Just go up to any animal and talk to them. You must talk to them first though otherwise they won't talk to you. There's Mr Tortoise. Go and talk to him" said the flower.

I still felt a bit silly but I went. "He's a bit deaf you will have to speak up Pedro" said the flowers. So I shouted "hello Mr Tortoise" "You don't have to shout I'm not deaf" said the tortoise. "But the flowers said you were a bit deaf." I said.

"Oh they are a bit mischievous. Look they are giggling"

"Oh sorry". "That's okay, whatever you are."

“I’m Pedro”.

“What’s a Pedro - some kind of animal I’ve never met?”

“No I’m a human and you’re an animal”.

“Poppycock! We are all the same fellow creatures.”

“I will start again. It’s nice to meet you Mr Tortoise have you lived here a long time?

“What’s a long time? “

“Well the time you have lived here” I said.

“I don’t know what you mean. We don’t have any of your time thing here. You talk such silly things. I must go, I’ve promised to help the frogs build a pond so they can have fun swimming. I expect I will see you again when you’re not so silly. Dig a hole and bury your silliness then you will be sensible. Good bye have a nice time with the frogs.”

This was such wonderful fun. Who can I talk to next I thought?

Manuel was still talking to the flowers so I went off to find others to talk to. There were so many fellow creatures about you could never ever get bored here. “Oh hello Mr Wolf are you having fun? I said.

“Yes he said.” I was a bit shocked I didn’t expect Mr Wolf to talk.

“Why didn’t you talk to me before” I said.

“Well I only could talk when I entered the valley” said the wolf.

“Manuel will be very pleased. He will love to talk to you. He likes you a lot”

“When I first came across Manuel I could tell he was a kind spirit but I could not talk to him then.” “This is wonderful. Let’s go and find our family and see if they can now talk just like you” I said.

CHAPTER 19

As we walked back along a beautiful flowery path a voice said “good morning”. As I looked about I saw a big green caterpillar on a tree branch. “Oh hello Mr Caterpillar how are you today?

“Very well thank you. I must dash. I have got to get changed into a butterfly. When I’m changed I will come and find you and we can finish our little talk”

“That would be lovely. But how will I know it’s you. There are so many butterflies about”. I said.

“Well I will land on your nose and say good morning again”

“I look forward to seeking you as a butterfly. Goodbye.

The caterpillar started up the tree towards the top. Mr Wolf and I carried on down the path and suddenly round a bend we stopped in our tracks. On the path in front of us was a huge brown bear. For a moment I was scared then I thought he is probably going to be nice like all the other creatures.

“Pedro do you remember me?

Then I suddenly realised it was the bear we let out of that awful circus cage.

“Did Manuel and I let you out of that cage?

“Yes you did and I’ve had so much lovely freedom since then.

“I’m so glad. Humans who put our fellow creatures in cages should be caged themselves. Every creature has the right to enjoy the freedom it was given in nature. It’s so nice to see you free and happy. Oh this is my friend Mr wolf.”

“It’s nice to meet you Mr Wolf.”

“Likewise Mr Bear.”

“Let’s go on and find our family. Would you like to be part of our family Mr Bear?” I said.

“That would be lovely Pedro. I can’t remember my family as I was a young bear when I was taken and put in a cage.”

“We will all make you happy Mr Bear and you will be free like us forever.”

As we carried on a little further I could hear Manuel and our family. “Hello Manuel. The last time I saw you, you were talking to those huge flowers. You must have come back here by a different path.”

“I was a bit lost and a little rabbit showed me the way back.”

Manuel saw Mr Bear and went over to him and hugged him. “I’m glad to see you Mr Bear.”

“Thank you for giving me my freedom. I will be your friend always.”

“Could you sit down Mr Bear so that our family can come to say hello. You look very big to them standing up.” I said.

“Oh, I forgot said Mr Bear. I also have a friend here called Lula. We met in the forest.

She was lost and I helped her and we are best friends"

"What's a Lula Mr bear" I said

"Here she is. Lula is my pug friend"

"Ah a little doggy hello Lula" I said. "This is our family Piggy, Messy, Peanut, Lucky, Matilda, Mr Wolf and Mr Bear. Will you be part of our family?

"Yes please.   It will be nice to have a loving family again"

"Oh and I'm Pedro and this is Manuel"

“You all look so happy” said Lula.

“Yes we are. It’s so wonderful here. You can almost feel the love and happiness” I said.

“I like Lula and I like little doggies” said Manuel.

“And I like you Manuel” said Lula. “You look nice and kind”

“Thank you. Will you be my friend Lula?

“Yes Manuel”.

It was another beautiful day and Mr Bear and Lula got to know us all.

Lula said Messy was sweet and so was everyone else but Messy was extra sweet !

“Oh sorry Mr Tortoise. I think we are blocking the path” I said.

We all stood aside and Mr Tortoise went past slowly with Mrs Tortoise and four baby tortoises. “Where are you going Mr Tortoise?

“Haven’t you heard the nice man in white wants to see everyone in the valley in the wide opening?”

Just then lots of fellow creatures were behind Mr Tortoise. I suppose off to see the man in white as well.

“We will follow you Mr Tortoise” I said.

CHAPTER 20

We all set off and wondered what he wanted of us all. From many different paths came hundreds of fellow creatures. We all moved into the wide opening in the valley and everyone was talking. It was quite a noise.

“Pedro what are we waiting for”?

“Well Manuel the nice man in white told us to come here and wait”.

Suddenly on a high rock there was a man in white sitting and looking down on us.

“I have come to take you all on a journey to the planet of peace which is looked after by the council of spirit elders who come from many different times and space dimensions. It is probably too much for you to understand but all with be revealed in time. Pedro. Manuel and your family come up here.” he said.

“How can we ? Its too high for us to climb” I said.

“Close your eyes tight then open them when I say” the man in white said.

We all closed our eyes. “Now open them” he said.

We opened our eyes. “How did we get here”? We were all on the rock next to the nice man in white.

“One day I will tell you so many wonders they can happen in a twinkling of an eye. When you and Manuel are ready one day I will show you worlds no human has ever seen and see things that will be beyond your wildest dreams but for now you will enjoy the planet of peace and all its wonders.”

Suddenly a loud voice shouted “STOP”!

As we looked down it was the police with some other people. “You’ve led us a long chase but we’ve found you come on down. The child welfare officer will take you and Manuel to a home for orphans”

The man in white said “do you want to go with them Pedro?

“No, no, no; we want to stay with you and be free to help our fellow creatures.”

“Don’t be silly said the police officer. Come down”

“You have your answer.” said the man in white.

Just then the police officer pulled out a gun. “I don’t know who you are but Pedro and Manuel are coming with us.”

The man in white pointed at the gun and it disappeared then another policeman pointed a gun and again the nice man made it vanish.

“Come Pedro and Manuel and your family follow me there through the rock”

“But we can’t go through solid rock” I said.

“Close your eyes” he said and again we did what he said.

“Now open them.” We opened our eyes.

“We couldn’t believe it. We were on the other side of the huge rock.

“Come a bit further and we will enter the planet of peace.”

“Please” I said. “What about all the other creatures that were left
Behind”?

He smiled. “They are not left - look!”

There they all were in front of us and as I looked back the valley was just a dry dust with some horrible people scratching their heads.

“Will they be able to get in here to take us away”?

“No Pedro that they will never be able to do.” said the man in white.

We walked down a long ramp into a world of such beauty the grass was so green and shiny; the sky was such a sparkling blue. The trees and flowers were much brighter than in the valley we had left. There were so many colourful birds and happy creatures chattering and playing everywhere before we could go any further the nice man said "Pedro you and Manuel were chosen to come here because of your innocence and great love of your fellow creatures.

"Did you choose us? I said.

"No you were chosen by the grand spirit to help and enjoy the planet of peace. In time you will see millions of fellow creatures throughout the universe and beyond to the final world of extreme beauty and light of the grand spirit so when it is time you will be called by the grand spirit to have incredible adventures. No one has ever dreamt of meeting the Grand Spirit, but that's all in the future." said the man in white.

"Excuse me but can we know your name; you know ours" I said.

He just smiled and said "we of the council of spirit elders have no need of names like you and Manuel but if you want to I am happy to have a name"

"Can Manuel and I choose one?

"Yes of course"

Manuel said “Can we call you uncle nice I’ve never had a nice uncle”?

“Of course. I don’t know what uncle nice is but it appears I now am one.”

He smiled and I said “come on there’s our family look over there. They are making so many new friends.”

“You will be back together soon” said the man in white.
As we walked along the track the surface sparkled in the bright light.

“What’s all that dust that sparkled uncle nice”?

“That’s pieces of gold and jewels” he said.

“If we took a bag full back to where we came from we would be rich.”

“Pedro you and Manuel can take as much as you want and go back to your world and be very rich but you would never be allowed back here because your innocence would be lost and earthly greed would set in. Is that what you and Manuel want?

I looked at all the beautiful animals and all the wonderful plants and trees of this lovely world. “No I want to stay here forever.”

“What about you Manuel? said the man.

“I want to stay with Pedro and you uncle nice”.

“Just a minute, Pedro”. Uncle nice stood still not moving then after a short time he spoke again. “That’s very good news Pedro. The grand spirit was talking to me and is very pleased you chose natures beauty over short term riches and greed.”

“I did not see anyone uncle nice”

“In our world we communicate by connecting our minds into one to talk through our minds over vast areas and space dimensions. All will be revealed to you and Manuel one day. Forget about all that for now, its time to show you the wonders of the Planet of Peace”.

Just then we heard “can we come too”? It was the rest of our family. Piggy, Messy, Lucky, Matilda, Lula, Peanut, Mr Wolf and Mr bear.

“Yes of course. Lets all go exploring.”

All of a sudden there were thousands of beautiful coloured birds flying around us and many landed on us. It was so lovely. Manuel loved birds and was so happy to touch them very gently.

"I am so happy Pedro. I love birds. They would come to our house when I was young and sad and would chirp and sing which made me happy again."

Birds landed on everyone. One landed on Mr Bear's nose which made him have a giant sneeze. Mr Wolf had lots on his back and said to them "Are you comfortable? "Yes we are" they said.

"Good it's nice to have you".

Messy had just one little bird on her back and loved it. Peanut held out his arms and more landed on them. Piggy, Lucky, Lula and Matilda had lots too. It looks like we have a much bigger family now. I hope there are no flying elephants about uncle nice!" I said.

He laughed. "Oh that's one thing we don't have and if we did and they landed on you, you would be rather flat".

CHAPTER 21

As we walked along the track it widened and round a bend we came to the sea. "Why don't you and Manuel have a swim and meet some more new friends? " He said.

The sea was the most beautiful blue and the water sparkled. The sand was a rich gold colour. I think it was real gold dust. "But uncle nice our clothes will get all wet." I said. "Just walk into the sea." He repeated.

So Manuel and I slowly walked into the sea. We could not believe it! Our clothes were all dry but we were in the sea. Uncle Nice why are our clothes dry? I said.

"If I had to explain all the things of this world it would take forever just enjoy a new adventure. We will wait here for you."

“But we can’t go into deep we can’t breath underwater Uncle Nice” I said.

“Trust me you can try it.”

I went under the water thinking I would get water in my mouth and up my nose but I could breathe just like on land. I popped up and shouted to Manuel. “We can breathe underwater Manuel” He came under the water and we walked along the sea. There were so many beautiful coloured fish, turtles and huge whales which were all different colours and so many other creatures. It was hard to take it all in. Just then a voice said

“I’ve never seen fish like you before”. It was a giant whale and he came up to us.

“We are not fish Mr Whale”

“So who are you. “

“Well I’m Pedro and this is Manuel” I said.

“What’s a Pedro and a Manuel?

“Well we are humans.”

“What’s a human?

“Humans live on the land and you live in the sea.”

“Oh, so are all creatures on land Pedro’s and Manuel’s? “

“No, humans have different names”.

“Like what? Said the whale.

“I don’t think I have enough time to explain it all Mr Whale. Let’s just enjoy getting to know each other.”

“Come along then and meet my good friend he likes everyone and puts his tentacles around you to show how much he likes you. I’ll just call him. Ah no need. Here he comes” said the Whale.

We saw a giant octopus. “Come and meet our new human fish” he said to the octopus. The octopus came over and put his tentacles all over us.

They were so soft and tickled Manuel and I started to laugh.

“What’s that noise” said the octopus. When someone puts there hands on your feet or parts of your body it makes you laugh.” I said.

“Can I tickle you Mr Octopus?”

“Well I suppose” he said.

So I reached out and put my fingers in his side and wiggled them about.

"Oh that's nice" he said.

"Manuel go and give Mr Whale a tickle" I said. So Manuel tickled Mr Whale's belly. They both gurgled loudly. That's fish giggling I thought. Well they seemed to enjoy it. Mr Whale said "We shall have to show our friends how to tickle we could have a tickle party. Thank you for showing us tickling Pedro and Manuel what else can you show us?"

“I don’t think we have time to show you any new things I hear Mr nice calling us. Come on Manuel we had better get back on land. Goodbye Mr Whale and Mr Octopus we will come again to see you.” I said.

“Yes do and I will show you all the wonders there are in the sea. Bye bye.”

Mr Nice’s voice said “Close your eyes”. We did as he said. “Now open them”. We were back on land. We should have been surprised but with all the wonders that had happened so far it all seemed so natural. Our family were glad to see us back on land. Lula walked to the sea. “Why don’t you go in and talk to the fishes Lula?

“No I don’t like wet water”.

“You won’t get wet. We didn’t!

“If I go in it will probably turn wet when I get in. When I was a puppy every time I went out in the sun a wet cloud would appear and wash me so I think I will just look thank you Pedro” said Lula.

“Come on said Uncle Nice. Off we go I’ve lots more still to show you.

“Are there dianasours”? I said. “You mean dinosaurs. Yes there are hundreds of different ones on a distant planet of giants Pedro.”

“Can we see them one day” I said. “All in good time. You see over there that big blue sun. That’s where we will go next.”

“Can we stop for a while uncle nice? I think we are all a bit tired it’s so wonderful here and so much for us to take in. “

“Of course”. I will leave you all for a short while. I have something to attend to for the Grand Spirit.”

“Okay uncle nice”.

“Pedro”? “Yes Manuel”

“I don’t feel hungry.
“No I don’t either and Piggy, Messy, Peanut, Lucky, Mr Wolf, Mr Bear and Lula all said they didn’t feel hungry. I will ask Uncle Nice when he gets back about that. “

We all lay down. Mr Bear lay down next to me and fell asleep.

“He’s snoring loudly like a snorerus”. I said.

“What’s a snorerus Pedro?” said Manuel.

“Well I don’t really know I think it’s someone with big loud snores.

“Oh okay”

We all snuggled up and fell asleep next to Mr Bear. When we woke up Uncle Nice was back and with a big smile on his face.

“Are you very happy Uncle Nice” “Yes Pedro the Grand Spirit sends his love to you all. We will meet him soon when the time is ready Pedro. First you must see some of all the wonders of the loving universe”

“Okay we will wait”. “Why are we not hungry uncle nice even Mr Bear’s tummy isn’t Rumbling?

“Where you have come to is the way all creatures should be towards their fellow creatures. Everyone has the right to enjoy there lives without fear of being eaten by another creature from an ant to an elephant. We all live in peace and harmony. We are all here to love and help one another and plants here can talk. Would you pick a flower and eat one Pedro?

"No that would not be kind"

"This is why your body does not need food here. Your bodies have all changed to the ways of the loving universe without the normal human cycle of greed and death. Its time we set off to meet the land of little creatures" said Uncle Nice.

“Will there be spiders there?” said Lula.

“Yes Lula but they are very kind ones”.

“That’s good because spiders frighten me” said Lula

Uncle nice laughed loudly. “Don’t worry Lula you will have a lovely time” said Uncle Nice.

CHAPTER 22

We walked for a short time when suddenly the ground changed. Instead of lovely shiny grass we were walking on very soft ground covered in silk. It was so lovely to walk on. "This is Great Uncle Nice" I said.

"Yes the spiders heard you were all coming so they made a silk path for you all".

I suddenly realised all my family had been very quiet.

"Are you all okay Mr Wolf, Matilda, Lucky, Peanut, Lula, Piggy,
Messy?

"Yes we are fine Pedro. We are just trying to take in all the wonders."

"You are quiet too Manuel" I said.

“Yes I want to stay here forever.

“You can” said Uncle Nice.   “You are all free to choose what you want to do.”

“We never want to go back” I said.

As we all walked on the silk path a rainbow mist appeared in front of us.

“We have arrived at the entrance to the land of little fellow creatures. Just walk through the mist with me”

We followed Uncle Nice. On the other side we found ourselves the same size as spiders.

“What happened uncle nice?

“You will find that your bodies will adapt to each new world you visit. I don’t expect you would like spiders your size would you?

“Ooh giant spiders! No thank you” said Lula.

Suddenly dozens of spiders of all colours came dangling down from the trees and flowers. They all said at once “hello to you all.”

“Are there only spiders here”? I said.

"No there are lots of other fellow insects" said Uncle nice. Here comes Mr Earwig"

As soon as that was said we all put our fingers in our ears. Uncle nice was grinning and laughing. "That's just their name. You can all take your fingers out of your ears" he said. Mr Earwig looked a bit puzzled. "Why would I want to get into your ears? How very silly. "

"Good morning Mr Spider said Mr earwig what a lovely day for doing nothing".

"I totally agree. Doing nothing is better than doing something you don't want to do." I said.

“I think we had better get on said uncle nice. Otherwise we will just all sit here doing nothing.”

“Can we come too said the spiders and Mr Earwig.”

“Yes of course said uncle nice. I don’t suppose Mr wolf , Mr Bear, Matilda, Peanut, Lucky, Messy, Lula and Piggy will mind you riding on their backs. “Hop on” said peanut but not too many. I’m only little”.

So the spiders came along with us even Manuel had some on his head and said “can you keep still spiders, you are tickling my head?"

As we rounded the corner Mr Earwig shouted out to his family "Come on we are going on an adventure."

"How many are coming Mr Earwig?

"I should think about enough to fill the top of your head Pedro".

Just then out of the silk flowers came Mr Earwig's' family. They were all very excited and climbed on my head. " It's funny because when I was living with Grandpa we used to pick up earwigs in the house and put them out into the garden, now I'm taking some for a trip on my head. Grandpa would laugh so much if he saw me now" I said. "Hold tight. Off we go". I said to the earwigs.

"Where are we going next uncle nice?

"We are off to ant town which is over there past the gold waterfall."

"Is it real gold water" I said.

"Yes Pedro and all the trees and bushes have gold fruit and berries on them but you can't eat them" said Uncle Nice. They are only there to delight the eye"

As we passed the waterfall we saw mounds of glass bits.

“That’s where the ants live Pedro said uncle nice.”

“Do they like glass”?

“That’s not glass Pedro. They are diamonds”

“Do you visit the ants very often Mr Earwig?” said Manuel.

“No, not as often as we would like to. You see we are so busy doing nothing we simply don’t have the time”

Suddenly there was a loud sound like a trumpet and hundreds of ants came out of the mounds.

“You are just in time for something or other” said the ants.

“What said Pedro”?

“Well something we haven’t done before you know. Nothing stuff”

I thought it best to agree with the ants otherwise we would be talking about nothing stuff forever. Uncle nice then said in my ear that the ants live in their own world.

“Its time for our show time” said the chief ant. Sit down all you er you er you whatever you all are”.

So our family and Uncle Nice made ourselves comfortable laying on gold grass and by plants of jewels and silver.

“What’s the play about” asked Mr Bear.

“It’s not a play it’s an antomime. We have shows when the spiders and others come by. We will now start”

There was a lovely sound of music I had never heard before.

“What is that Uncle Nice ? I said.

“It’s the sounds of nature in harmony with all creatures. Every planet we will visit has total harmony of love and happiness. The world you came from Pedro has lost its way in everything that is right and good. In your world is the human obsession for more wealth and power”.

“Can we get on” said the ant.

“Oh sorry Mr Ant” said Uncle Nice.

The antomime went on with music juggling and dancing. There was no singing as the ants didn’t have good singing voices.

As we watched suddenly lots of other fellow insects came along there were ladybirds, beetles, worms, earwigs. “Can we watch? They all said.

“Of course. Sit where you like”. So they all spread out amongst us. The ladybirds sat with Lucky and Peanut, the worms sat with Messy, the beetles sat with Mr Wolf and Mr Bear and the earwigs with Piggy.

“Oh what fun” said Mr Bear. “I haven’t had so much fun since the last time I didn’t have so much fun I think.”

“Are you enjoying the show Manuel?

“Yes Pedro. I feel so happy since we left all the nasty people behind and all the lovely new friends we have. Its had been a fantastic day.”

The ants had finished their show and laid down for a snooze. We were all getting a bit tired so we all had a snooze.

“Are you going to have a snooze Uncle Nice ?

“No Pedro you all have a rest I am planning your next adventure.”

“What’s that? I said.

“You will have to wait and see Pedro”

When we woke up Uncle Nice said “I am taking you all to the Planet of Giants”

“How do we get there?

“Well Pedro. It’s easy. Everyone close your eyes tight; all hold hands and paws now count to three and open your eyes. One, two, three.

When we opened our eyes we realised we were very much bigger than we were.

“Why are we so big uncle nice said Manuel?

“That’s because you are on the Planet of Giants but don’t be worried because all the fellow creatures you will meet are loving soft and kind. While you are on this planet you will stay big until we leave. As we looked around flowers of such beauty were as tall as trees and strange huge birds were everywhere. One landed in front of us.
“Good morning” I said.

“Oh good morning Mr Bird” said Peanut. “Are you visiting us on the way to see the Grand Spirit?

“Yes I think its best to ask Uncle Nice”. I said.

"Who is Uncle Nice" said the bird.

"They all decided to call me Uncle Nice" said the Spirit Elder.

"We all know you as one of the spirit elders and your visits to us are always welcome.
"Come on everyone lots of us are to meet in the wide place".

"Pedro you and Manuel are very quiet." said Uncle Nice.

"Well we were wondering why we have quick visits to all these wonderful worlds"

“Well Pedro” said Uncle Nice. “There are so many planets to see before you meet the Grand Spirit we have to make them short visits but after you have seen some of the wonders of the universe and had time with the Grand Spirit you will be free to roam and visit and stay as long as you all like in your favourite world. Do you all intend to stay together Pedro?

“I hope so Uncle Nice”

“Would you like to stay together as a family” I asked everyone and they all shouted, “Yes, forever and ever”.

Manuel was so happy to hear that and so was I.

“Come on off we go to the wide place” said Uncle Nice.

CHAPTER 23

We followed the big bird through a forest of trees with leaves of all colours. The tree bark was so soft and as I touched the bark a voice said “that tickles.”!

“Who said that uncle nice”?

“Why, the tree of course Pedro.” The flowers, trees and all your fellow creatures here can talk.”

“Mr Tree do you like being a tree? I said.

"Yes because I'm not keen on exercise so being a tree suits me."

"I agree said a huge flower. I like to stand here swaying in the wind and watching the world go by."

"Oh okay" I said.

"If you stand here long enough you might root in the ground and be a tree like me"

"I'm sure its nice being a tree but I like walking and exploring but thanks for the offer Mr Tree." I said.

“Come on” said Uncle Nice. “We are nearing the wide place.”

There were a few huge bushes to go past and then the most fantastic view opened up. There were so many big fellow creatures in front of us and prehistoric creatures of all kinds as far as the eye could see. Everywhere there were grasses of gold bushes covered in jewels, mountains covered in flowers of such beauty and there was a huge lake so blue it was so hard to describe the wonder of it. Everything was so bright but it didn’t hurt your eyes.

“Is it safe to walk down to see all our huge fellow creatures’ uncle nice” I said.

“Of course Pedro.” “They are all nice soft and loving. Come on Pedro, Manuel and everyone let me take you to meet them.”

There were so many it would take a long time to say hello to all of them. “It’s so lovely to see you again Mr and Mrs Softiesaurus” said uncle nice.

“Likewise to you”

Mr and Mrs Softiesaurus looked over to us and said “Are you all freshly made? “We’ve never seen creatures like you all before “

Uncle nice laughed. “No they are not freshly made they are from another world called earth”

“Have you come to live here”?

“No I don’t think so” I said.

“They are on a journey to meet the Grand Spirit and I’m showing them some of the wonders of a happy universe and beyond to the majestic land of the Grand Spirit” said Uncle Nice.

There were lots of other lovely creatures wanting to say hello.

“I’m Lazysnoozeasaurus”

“How do you spell that? I said.

“I don’t know. I’ve never been asked before. I will ask Mr Nicealotorus”.

“I’ve no idea.” he said. “Let’s ask Mr Hippyasaurus”

“I think we had better forget about the spelling” said Uncle Nice. “By the time you have asked everyone we will be here forever.”

“Quite so” said a voice from under the ground.

“Who’s that” I said.

“It’s just me, Giganticmoleasarus”.

“He likes to live under the ground. Goodness knows why it’s much nicer up here” said Mr Hippyosaurus.

“Goodbye everyone said Mr Giganticmolesaurus. “I’m off to see something you don’t see every day but I’m not sure what it is. Oh well must dash”.

The ground shook as he burrowed away.

“He’s always looking for something you don’t see every day but he never finds it” said Mr Hippyasaurus.

Just then a small creature came up to us and brushed against us and it looked very happy.

“What’s that? Said Mr Wolf

“That’s Mr and Mrs Hugemungasaurus’ son. He’s lovely and so sweet they call him Bonzo”

“You all seem to have funny names here” I said.

“And why not” said Mr Hugemungasaurus. “It’s better than having an unhappy name like Mr Verygrumpyoldasaurus or Mr Moaneyasaurus”

“Can we all play with baby Bonzo?

“Yes of course; he would like some new friends.” said Mr Hugemungasaurus.

“All enjoy yourselves for a while” said Uncle Nice. “I’m going to take a snooze”.

Peanut climbed onto baby Bonzo and they both had big smiles on their faces. “Let’s have a race. The first one to that big rock over there wins” I said. So we all lined up. “

ONE-TWO-THREE – go !" We all ran. Messy was hanging onto baby Bonzo's tail. Lucky, Matilda, Lula and Piggy were getting puffed out.

Mr Wolf could have easily won but I think he wanted our new friend baby Bonzo to win. Mr Bear was a way behind huffing and puffing. "I'm too old to run" he said. Baby Bonzo and Peanut and Messy reached the rock first. Manuel and I came second and we were all out of breath so we all sat on the big flat rock.

"Excuse me" said a voice. "There are too many of you sitting on me."

“Who’s that” said Manuel. “It’s me of course!   “Who’s me?

“Me is who you are sitting on” said the rock.

We suddenly all realised it was the rock that was talking.

“I’ve never heard of a rock talking” said Mr Bear. “Nor me” said Mr Wolf.

“I don’t know where all you new strange creatures have come from but we all talk here. Just a minute I forgot to say good morning to Mr Mountain over there. Good morning Mr Mountain”

“Hello Mr rock. Lovely day isn’t it? “Yes it’s another wonderful day.”

“What do you think of these strange new creatures” said Mr Rock.

Mr Mountain paused. “I think they will fit in nicely here; they all seem to fit in our jolly world. Do you all think so rocks? There was a huge sound of lots of voices shouting. “Yes they will all fit in nicely.”

It was all the other rocks welcoming us.

“Uncle nice it’s so lovely. Can we stay and live here?

"As I said to you before Pedro we are making a quick tour of some of the wonderful worlds of the universal dimension. When you have met the Grand Spirit and listened to his plan for you, you will be able to travel anywhere and visit and stay as long as you want. That's also includes Manuel and your family"

"I can't wait to meet the Grand Spirit"

"Good" said uncle nice.

"I've been thinking. What happened to all the nasty people who hurt animals and people young and old? I said.

“They will not be able to enjoy our beautiful world” said Uncle Nice.

“That’s a shame. Maybe they will turn into nicer people one day” I said.

“Let’s play hide and seek” I said. Will you play Uncle Nice?

“Well Spirit Elders don’t usually play games but yes why not.
I don’t know what the grand spirit will make of all this but I’m sure he will enjoy watching us. He has the loving heart and the kindness of a child”.

“We will go and hide. Baby Bonzo, you should close your eyes and count to 20 and we will shout ready and you can come and find us. It will take some time to find us all. Is that okay Baby Bonzo ?” I said.

“Yes Pedro that’s sounds like great fun I’ve never played with so many lovely friends before.”

We all found a place to hide. “Count to 20 Baby Bonzo”.

Manuel and I hid behind Mr Rock. Matilda and Lucky found some very tall gold grass to hide in and uncle nice hid behind Mr Gigantomoleasorus. Peanut, Piggy and Messy found a tree to hide behind and Mr Bear, Mr Wolf and Lula hid behind Mr and Mrs Softiesaurus who were delighted to help with the game and we all shouted "ready Baby Bonzo !".

Dozens of other fellow creatures came to watch. It must have been something they had never seen before. Baby Bonzo looked down the Enormousbunnyasaurus' burrow. "Are you in there? He said. An echo came back "Not today thank you"

That didn't sound right so Baby Bonzo tried again. "Are you in?

“I’m not in today or tomorrow thank you or yesterday” said the voice.

We were all laughing. I think Mr Enormousbunnyasourus was joining in with the game too. “Oh this is silly” said Baby Bonzo. “I’ll look over by the rocks. “Mr Rock do you know where they are all hiding?

“I can’t tell you exactly where they are but you are getting close”. Said the Rock.

Just then Manuel sneezed and Baby Bonzo soon found us behind Mr Rock.

“Ah found you. Where are all the others Pedro?

“They are hiding in different places you will have to look for them all”

Baby Bonzo walked towards Mr and Mrs Softiesaurus.” Ha I found you! “Where shall I look next? I know I wonder if anyone is behind Mr Giganticmoleasurus mound.” Baby Bonzo peeked round the mound and shouted “found you”. It made Uncle Nice jump. I think he was snoozing again.

Baby Bonzo carefully looked behind to find as many creatures as possible but nobody was there. “I’ll try the golden grass meadow” thought Baby Bonzo. As he walked by the meadow he could see a white tail sticking out of the grass. That's not grass he thought and he pulled it. "Ouch" a voice said. "That's my tail". "Got you" said Baby Bonzo. "Who is left? "Just Peanut, Piggy and Messy".

Baby Bonzo looked all over the place. "I'm tired now" said Baby Bonzo. I will rest under this tree. Can I rest against you Mr Tree?

"Of course my little friend make yourself comfy"

"I wish I could find Peanut, Piggy and Messy" said Baby Bonzo.

"Close your eyes" said Mr tree "and count to three"

“Okay ONE – TWO- THREE!”

Mr Tree then shook his leaves and branches and Peanut, Piggy and Messy fell out of the tree onto Baby Bonzo. Everyone was laughing so loud at this sight it sounded like a volcano bursting.

“When I’m rested can we do some more? said Baby Bonzo.

“Not for now” said Uncle Nice. “Its time for us to carry on to another world but we will all come back again”. Don’t worry Baby Bonzo we will be back.” said Uncle Nice.

“Can I come with you all” said Baby Bonzo.

“Well I suppose you could say Uncle Nice. “What do you all think?

We all said yes that would be lovely to have Baby Bonzo as another member of our family” I said.

“Let’s go and ask Mr and Mrs Hugemungasaurus if that’s okay.”

“Baby Bonzo wants to come with us Mr and Mrs Hugemungasaurus”

“Well he’s quite a big boy now and not such a big baby anymore, so yes we think its fine we know he will be safe with you”.

“He will be back after we meet the grand spirit” said Uncle Nice.

So Baby Bonzo who is a big boy now said goodbye to his mum and dad.

“Are you all ready” said Uncle Nice.

“Yes thank you” we all said.

“Walk with me over to that rainbow and when we get to the end of it follow me” said Uncle Nice.

CHAPTER 24

We walked up and over to it.

"But will it take all our weight Uncle Nice?" I said.

"Yes of course Pedro. Hello Rainbow" said uncle nice. "How are you?

"Very colourful thank you"

"Good. Can we come and cross over on you now"

"Yes it will be nice to have some visitors"

"It's always polite to ask first Pedro" said uncle nice. Even though we can just cross over anyway. Come on off we go".

We followed Uncle Nice and stepped onto the rainbow.

“Oh” said the rainbow. “That tickles. I’m not used to such a lot of travellers but its okay being tickled its quite nice”.

We all kept climbing over the rainbow. Uncle nice was in front and as we reached the peak of the rainbow we saw a huge cloud. It came over to us.

“Hello Mr cloud” said uncle nice. You are on time as usual”.

“We cloud taxis have to be otherwise there would be a huge queue.”

"Now let me see" said Mr Cloud. "I will have to wait for a second while you get back to your normal size"

Just then we all realised we were our normal size again.

"Why have we gone back to normal Uncle Nice" I said.

"Well if you were still a giant size as you were, Mr Cloud couldn't take us all to where we are going"

"Oh I see" I said.

Uncle nice looked back to see if we were all together. “Are you ready to step onto Mr Cloud everyone”?

We all said yes except for Mr Bear.

“If we all step onto Mr Cloud we will fall through?” said Mr Bear.

“No don’t worry Mr Bear it’s all very safe. “

As we started to get onto Mr Cloud he changed his shape and big soft fluffy chairs appeared.

“Now sit down everyone and make yourselves comfortable.” said the cloud.

"The seats are lovely" said Peanut and Lula and we all agreed with that.

"Where are we going uncle nice" said Mr Cloud. "What planet are we going to"?

"Its time for a tour of the galaxy". "There are millions of planets in this part of the eternal cosmos."

"Does the cosmos have an end like a brick wall"?

"No Pedro there is no end it goes on forever into galaxies with worlds of such wonder and beauty. It would be at the moment impossible for you to understand that is something the grand spirit will show you."

Just then Uncle Nice stood still and shut his eyes. We all kept quiet as we didn't know what was happening. His eyes opened.

"I have a message for you all from the Grand Spirit. He says he will have a wonderful surprise for you all after he meets you".

"When will that be? Said Manuel.

"When the time is ready"

“Mr Cloud lets go through the cosmic space mist to take a flying tour of the planets of the sparkling light” said Uncle Nice.

As we entered the mist lovely sounds were heard nothing like music on earth. It was so calming it seemed to touch your body and made you feel so wonderfully happy.

“It tickles my hair” said Mr Wolf. “And mine” said Mr Bear.

“How does the mist do all these lovely things Uncle Nice? I said.

“Well, Pedro the mists are loving creatures. I know it’s hard for you to understand but simple little specks of space dust are travelling through the mist and it causes sounds and then the mist makes more music from it. We call it galactic harmony in tune with the universe."

Suddenly we came out of the mist and everything was so bright and sparkly. There were lights of all colours flying around us.

"What are they uncle nice? I said.

"These are the light creatures from the bright planet below us" he said.

"But they aren't creatures Uncle Nice just swirling lights".

"Well Pedro they are creatures of the cosmos. The same as you and Manuel. It will be very hard for you to understand all you will see as we travel but at the end of our travels you will have the knowledge to know the never ending wonders of the endless time and space. Just enjoy the creatures of light. Talk to them Pedro and all of you as well they will love that and like to play."

"Piggy, Messy, Bonzo, Peanut, Lucky, Lula, Matilda, Mr Wolf and Mr Bear" "said Uncle Nice. "Have some fun. Call the light creatures to play with you."

We all said "Please come and play with us".

Suddenly there were little lights all around us flying about sparkling and changing colour. They all covered Mr Cloud and us with lovely warming lights they were all over Mr Bear. He looked like a Christmas tree with all the decoration on it and Peanut was covered in so many lights it was hard to see him. A light landed on Baby Bonzo's nose and it made him look like a Christmas reindeer.

As they flew around they made lovely soft sounds like a dove cooing.

"Uncle nice you said we should talk to them but they are only sparkling lights" I said.

“Well ask them what you like” he said.

As more soft lights landed on me I said hello expecting no reply but they said “what is hello?

“Well” I said. “It’s when we meet someone we greet them with hello”

“Hello hello hello hello” the lights started saying over and over again then uncle nice said “I think its better if you stick to one word like hello otherwise we will be here forever teaching the light creatures your language.”

"It all still feels like an incredible dream and I might wake up soon and all the wonders we have seen" I said.

"No it's not a dream Pedro" said Uncle Nice. "And there are still millions of planets and fellow creatures that will be a wonder to you all and as you now have eternal life if you stay, you will have so much time to travel in the eternal universe." He said.

"What would happen if we wanted to go back to earth?

"Well you, like all other creatures on earth, live until you get old and then fade away like the dust of the earth."

“I just wondered what would happen but I would never go back. What about you all?

“No never”! They all replied.

Lots of light creatures landed on uncle nice and he started to talk to them in their normal cooey language.

“We’ve been invited to land on the planet of lights” said uncle nice. “So hold tight. Can you take us down to the planet Mr Cloud?

“Yes. Off we go. Hold on”

“Whoosh down we flew at high speed. The light creatures seemed to love this and they started to make giggling sounds.

“That’s when they are happy and having fun” said uncle nice.

CHAPTER 25

We soon landed on their planet and everywhere were the most beautiful colours. We were all looking in amazement and we did not notice that there were hundreds of creatures like us but were made of so many colours.

“Hello Pedro and your friends” said the colourful creatures in front of me.

“Hello what happened to the small light figures in the sky with us” I said.

“That’s us said the creatures. When we leave our planet to go into space we change into small colourful pieces so we can float and fly like a feather and when we come back to our planet all the small pieces come back together to make us what you see now.”

“Do you have a name? I said.

“No we are all one light creation so we have no need of names”.
“It’s all so much again to take in Uncle Nice” I said.

“It will all become clear soon Pedro.”

“Come along everyone” said the light creatures. Follow us and we will show you some of our planet”.

As we all set off so did hundreds of other light creatures. They walked behind us happily singing some sort of strange sound and they were all wearing big colourful smiles. There was what looked like an escalator travelling across the ground for everyone to hop on.

We all got on. It was strange. It was a moving pathway and the light creatures were quiet now and they seemed to be delighted in watching us marvel at their world. As the pathway moved us along we could see meadows of flowers; all with the most wonderful colours and all the ground was covered in so many colourful petals.

“Do you have animal creatures on your planet” I asked the light creature who was leading the tour.

“I don’t understand. What are they?

“Well, like my family except for Manuel.”

“Oh I see. No we don’t have anything like those they are not colourful enough for our planet.”

There were blue petals floating past us. It looked like a stream but as I touched it they were just petals.

“Sorry to stop things” said uncle nice. “But we must move on again.”

“Oh that’s a shame” said the light creature. “But you can all come back anytime to see us.”

“Yes they will one day.” said Uncle Nice.

“Manuel looked dazed. “Are you okay Manuel? I said.

"Yes fine Pedro. It's all the colours I have been staring at. They have made my eyes go funny."

All our family looked a bit dazed.

"You are not used to new lights and colours" said uncle nice. "Lets move over there and go through the veil of silk and your eyes will get back to normal. We are now going to go through the veil to the great pathway to the grand spirits world."

"Wow at last Manuel. We are going to see the Grand Spirit." I said.

“Yes” said Uncle Nice. “The time has come to visit his world. Is everyone here Pedro?

“Let me see. Yes all here.”

As we went through the huge veil of silk I saw a long path of the brightest green I have ever seen and it seemed to go on and on and all around there were flowers of so many colours and their scent was so wonderful.

“This scent reminds me of my mother Sophia. She made scent from roses. I miss her still” said Manuel.

“Look Manuel by the roses; red and yellow honeysuckle. Grandpa Joseph used to grow lots of that. We both miss them Manuel" I said.

"Is it far to the grand spirit now Uncle Nice? I said.

"No, not far now."

Flowers either side of the path were so beautiful and they had smiles on their plant faces. Uncle nice stopped.

"Now standstill a minute" he said.

Suddenly the sky was full of small birds of so many lovely colours. They flew down onto the flowers and started to sing the most beautiful sounds. They were so calming and sweet. We were so happy looking at the birds we hadn't noticed the green path had come to an end.

"Oh where do we go now Uncle Nice?

"Just follow me and do as I do"

In front was a lake covered with gigantic lily pads.

"Come" said Uncle Nice. He stepped onto the lily pads and started to walk on top of them. We all stopped at the edge.   Uncle Nice looked round.

“Come on off we go” he said.

“Some of us are very big and heavy and we will fall in.”

Uncle nice laughed. “You should trust me by now Pedro. Would I let you get into any danger?

“No uncle nice”.

“I will l go first” said Manuel. As he stepped onto the lily it was fine.

“It’s like a soft path of leaves Pedro.” So we all started to follow Uncle Nice.

I had expected to see grand palaces in the Grand Spirit's world but it was so far just the most beautiful plants and birds and nature as far as the eye could see.

"When we get to that huge blue lily pad Pedro all hold hands and paws and claws and hold onto each other. Hold my hand Pedro. Is everyone holding each other?

"Yes we all are."

As he stepped onto the huge blue lily he started to fly and soon we were all flying up and over mountains of sparkling glass. As we looked down there were children playing and singing in fields of the most beautiful flowers. All the children looked up and waved to us. As we carried on we could see valleys and plains with more children playing and there was such beauty everywhere. It made earth look dull.

“Does the Grand Spirit live in a big castle Uncle Nice?

“No Pedro there aren’t any castles or palaces. Everyone lives amongst the natural world.” said Uncle Nice.

“Hold on. We are going down after the next mountain.”

As we flew over it, down below we could see what looked like a huge garden full of the most beautiful plants and trees of all colours it was so bright uncle nice said “we will land over by the wisdom tree. Here we go.”

Down on the ground again we were all standing under a gigantic tree. Its bark was like velvet and every leaf was so colourful. “Pedro can you and Manuel and all your family sit over there by the stream of wonder. This is what I have brought you all this way for. Now you will meet the Grand Spirit.”

Suddenly from behind the tree a figure appeared surrounded by veils of such bright colour and Uncle Nice went over and he and the figure just looked at each other. They did not speak for a short while. We all looked on in wonder.

“Pedro, Manuel come over here. The Grand Spirit now wishes to talk to you”

As we got up to go over to the figure surrounded by veils so bright, they suddenly vanished and standing in front of us was a man whose face was of such beauty and kindness we felt so happy and safe by him. He spoke.

“I expect you were thinking before you met me that I would be like a prince or king covered in gold and jewels.” He said.

“Yes sir”.

He laughed. “I’m not a Sir or anything like that. We are all one and nobody is better than anyone else. We live together in such happy harmony with the natural world all around us as in the other planets. The Spirit Elder or uncle nice as you call him took you to the trees, plants, mountains, rocks, streams and animals and they all talk just like I am now”.

“Will we see lots more children and animals” I said.

“Yes they are everywhere. You will soon see and meet thousands of them in your travels in our world and other worlds." said the Grand Spirit.

"Why did you bring us here" I said.

"I have been looking for someone like you and Manuel who have a totally pure heart for the natural world. I've been searching for hundreds of your earth years".

"But you only look young" I said.

He smiled. "It is hard for you to understand but I have been in the universe forever helping loving creatures to live in a world away from the greed and destruction of your world and although I have the spirit elders to communicate with it would be nice to have a helper to see that the new arrivals of children and animals are welcomed”.

“Do you send for them?”

“No they arrive after their lives were cut short on your earth. They can then come here and be happy forever.” said the Spirit.

“Will they grow up here?”

“No Pedro they will stay as children always; so would you and Manuel like to help me?”

“Yes please” we both said.

“Now your family of fellow creatures what would you like to do”?

“Can we all stay here with Pedro and you?”

“Yes of course. You are now free to wander everywhere and to explore and meet new loving happy fellow creatures”.

“We all have names” I said. So do you have one Mr Spirit?”

“No we all communicate by thoughts from our minds. You can now do the same if you try it.”

I looked at Mr Spirit and suddenly I could talk to him through my mind.

“That’s so strange” I said.

“Don’t worry Pedro you can still talk as normal to everyone. You can do either.

“Mr Spirit?” said Manuel.

“Yes Manuel?”

“It’s so lovely here but I still feel very sad sometimes. You see I wish my mother was here with us all and I really miss my grandpa too”

“Well” said Mr Spirit. “Who is that over there?” We both cried with total delight it was Grandpa Joseph and Sophia, Manuel’s mother.

“Are they real Mr Spirit?”

“Of course they are. Very real. Go to them they will be here with you forever. And you will also see your mother and father soon Pedro.”

With tears running down our faces we ran to them and hugged them tight we had so much to tell each other. We looked back to see the rest of our animal family looking sad. “Don’t worry said Mr Spirit I haven't forgotten you all. Turn around."

There were all our animal families' mums and dads as well. Now we can all be happy forever. One day all the fellow creatures with pure hearts will come here to enjoy this wonderful happy loving world forever.

Love Pedro, Manuel, Mr Wolf, Mr Bear, Lula, Baby Bonzo, Matilda, Peanut, Lucky, Messy and Piggy. xxx

THE END?

No it's just the beginning! Now let your imagination take over!

Travel throughout the universe. What amazing wonders you will see!

Printed in Great Britain
by Amazon